DEATH BEFORE DESSERT

A Vanessa Harrington Cozy Mystery

A.E. RADLEY

D0168156

DEATH BEFORE DESSERT

1

NOT IN LONDON ANYMORE

"Tickets, please!"

Clara Harrington jumped at the bellowed request from the train conductor, who had suddenly appeared beside her. She looked along the empty carriage and wondered if it was really necessary for him to shout quite so loudly when she was the only person on board.

She lowered her book to her lap and dug her hand into her jeans pocket to seek out her ticket.

"That's seen better days," the conductor said, tilting his head towards Clara's bike. The 1955 Rudge Ulster Tourist had indeed seen better days, but Clara had lovingly repaired it since it came into her possession five years ago. Installation of the new leather saddle and handlebar grips were something she took personal pride in.

She'd never considered herself a handy kind of person, but through the magic of YouTube and trial and error she had transformed the bike from scrap metal to a viable method of transportation.

"It's just as good as any modern bike," she informed the

conductor, pulling her ticket out of her pocket and handing it to him.

He made a grand performance of checking it before validating it with his hand-held punch pliers.

"Picklemarsh, eh?" He handed her back the ticket.

"Yes." Clara put the ticket back in her pocket. She picked up her book and hoped that would be an end to the conversation.

"Not many people stop there," he said, obviously itching for more chitchat.

I'm really not in London anymore, Clara thought to herself.

From the quiet and dated train to the chatty conductor and ticket sellers, never had the city felt so far away. Even if she was only in rural Buckinghamshire just two hours away by car.

"I'm visiting my aunt," she explained, her nose still buried in her book in the hope that the man would take the hint and go about his work. He'd already needlessly shouted in her ear and then insulted her bike; she would hate to see what he had planned for an encore.

"Three stops away," he told her, seemingly taking the hint.

"Thank you," she said, unable to be rude and completely ignore him.

"You play?" His foot pointed to the violin case she held safely between her boots.

"I do."

"I like that... what do you call it?" He leaned against the back of the chair opposite Clara and looked up at the ceiling deep in thought. "You know, that famous violin guy."

"Nigel Kennedy?" She guessed; it was the only violinist many people could name. Especially British people of a certain age.

"Him and that Vivalto, very good."

"Vivaldi," she corrected.

"Yes, that. I loved that. Anyway, have a nice holiday with your aunt." He turned and walked back into the other carriage of the train.

Her old commute had trains of eleven carriages arriving every ten minutes, and there still wasn't enough room for the crowds of people waiting on the busy platform to board. Here, the train had two carriages, and Clara had one entirely to herself. Sheer luxury. The possibility of even getting a *seat* was usually considered fanciful in London.

She closed her eyes and leaned her head back against the headrest. It would be good to get away from London for a while. Especially as she was technically unemployed and homeless at the moment.

Her heartrate picked up, and she took a couple of deep breaths to calm herself down. She'd been wise and kept a savings account topped up. She had enough money to take a short break from work and then get back to the real world when she felt better.

Whenever that might be. She'd never been so stressed and frazzled before. "Burned out" was what one of her friends had called it. She'd never really thought of herself gradually burning out; she'd just been living her life and doing all the things that were necessary. All the things that were expected of someone these days.

Somewhere along the line, it had all fallen apart.

She'd never been to Picklemarsh, and Google had been

extremely unhelpful. Apparently, it was too small for the world's biggest search engine to really bother with.

Her aunt had moved there three years ago, having had enough of rattling around in her large London house. Vanessa hadn't spoken much about her new home and village life, only saying that Clara would have to visit and find out for herself. Since then, Clara had often been invited for a visit but had never had the time.

Until the day she was suddenly sacked from her job when the business folded overnight. To say it had been a surprise was an understatement. Not that Clara had enjoyed the job, just that it had become a part of her life. And suddenly, it was gone.

That evening she had called her aunt, who was always a wealth of knowledge and common sense, and advised her that her life was over. Clara explained that she had no job, and that her lease was ending, as her landlord had decided to sell up.

There was no way another landlord would give her a lease without employment. Aunt Vee had the obvious solution. "Well then, my dear," she said, "now seems like as good as time as any to come and visit your dear old Aunt Vanessa."

ARRIVING AT PICKLEMARSH

"Can I help you, Miss?"

Clara was struggling to remove her bike, two suitcases, and violin case from the train and was grateful for the help, even if it did come from a young man in an ill-fitting uniform. Clara thought station attendants had disappeared years ago, but apparently not in Picklemarsh.

"Oh, yes, please. Could you take Charity?"

The station attendant's hands remained outstretched and willing to help, though there was confusion in his eyes.

"Oh! Sorry, I mean my bike. I call her Charity. She was a gift," Clara explained.

The attendant grabbed the bike from the train's doorway and easily hoisted it onto the platform.

"Nice, is it original?" he asked, turning and taking both of the suitcases out of her hands to place them on the platform.

"It is. I did her up myself." Clara picked up her violin case and disembarked from the train.

"I think my granddad used to have one of these," he said, still admiring the bike.

"They are from the fifties; you can tell how well they were made by the fact that so many of them are still around."

"I upcycle furniture in my spare time," the attendant said. "My parents have a shop in the high street, and now and then they'll let me have a corner to sell things. It's fun, and it's helping the environment."

"I'll have to look out for the shop. What's it called?"

"Milton Furnishings." He proffered a hand. "I'm Edward Milton. We're not very original with our shop names around here, I'm afraid."

Clara chuckled and took his hand. "At least you know who owns what, I suppose."

Edward looked up and down the platform. "One second," he said. He lifted his whistle to his lips and blew hard twice to indicate to the driver that all the passengers were clear. All two of them. A few moments later the train doors closed, and the engine slowly pulled away from the platform.

"Is someone picking you up, or will you need a taxi?" Edward asked, looking at all of Clara's belongings.

"I'll need a taxi," she said. "I'm guessing you don't have Uber around here?"

Edward laughed. "Nah, not around here. I'll call Big Dave. He's the local taxi driver."

"You just have one?" Clara asked in surprise.

"Never needed more than one," Edward admitted. He jutted his thumb towards the station. "I'll give him a tinkle; I'll be back in a minute to help you with your bags."

"That's kind, but I can manage," Clara said, not used to the assistance.

Edward gestured around the empty platform. "There's not another train for fifty minutes, I have nothing else to do. You'll be doing me a favour, so I don't fall asleep from boredom!"

"Okay, that's really helpful. Thank you."

"Oh, where are you heading?" Edward asked as an afterthought.

"Chadwick... something," Clara replied, trying to recall the exact address her aunt had given her.

Every scrap of pleasantness fell from Edward's face. "Chadwick? You're not *a* Chadwick, are you?"

Clara frowned and quickly shook her head. "Um. No. I'm a Harrington, actually."

"Oh!" The smile returned to his face in a flash. "Chadwick *Lodge*. Are you a relative of Miss Harrington?"

"Yes, she's my aunt," Clara replied, wondering what on earth was wrong with being a Chadwick. Whoever they were, they were not popular with Edward Milton. The change in his disposition had been quite the surprise.

"I'll call Big Dave," Edward said, a spring back in his step as he walked to the station building.

Big Dave turned out to be a skinny man called Terry. Clara didn't ask why. In fact, she didn't get a chance to ask why, as she was quizzed for her life story the moment she sat in the back of Terry's Prius.

If she needed any further reminders that she was no

longer in London, the seven-minute journey from the train station to Chadwick Lodge was it.

Dave, or rather Terry, asked about her journey, her visit, her bike (which was attached haphazardly to the roof rack), her two suitcases, her violin, and her choice in music. The last was part of a gracious act in allowing her to choose between the two radio stations which, owing to the place being in a bit of a ditch, could successfully be picked up in the village of Picklemarsh.

She had a choice between Damian FM, which was run by a local teenager from his bedroom, and Picklemarsh FM. Damian FM seemed to specialise in the kind of angry heavy metal that stemmed from being a bored teen stuck in a town that was located in a ditch. Picklemarsh FM was currently not operating as the owner was on holiday in Cornwall.

Clara opted for silence.

She realised she'd made a grave error once Terry felt the need to fill the silence with endless questions.

"Here we are," he finally said as they rounded a corner at the end of a narrow road.

They pulled up outside a beautifully quaint cottage. A small, iron gate led into a perfectly kept garden which included roses and buddleia. Ivy covered the house, which was the kind of building Clara used to draw as a child: a large rectangle, four windows, a door in the middle.

A car horn sounded loudly, breaking the peace.

"Yeah, yeah! Keep your hair on!" Terry shouted out of the open window. He put the Prius into reverse, and they backed up a little.

Clara saw an expensive-looking black car pass them. The male driver looked to be in his fifties and stared at Terry with disdain. He drove around the taxi and through a large, open metal gate beside the cottage before proceeding up the driveway and out of sight.

"Does he live there?" Clara asked.

"No. He wishes. That's Julian Bridgewater, probably going to see Lord Muck himself."

"Lord Muck?"

"Angus Chadwick," Terry replied. "He owns Chadwick Manor, up that driveway. Your aunt lives in Chadwick Lodge; it used to be the gatekeeper's lodge many years ago. It was converted about eighty years ago, and now they rent it out."

Terry opened his door and pulled his lanky frame out of the vehicle. He opened the rear passenger door for Clara.

"Thank you," she said.

"Finally!" a familiar voice called from the cottage door. "I thought I'd have to wait until my funeral to see you again!"

Clara rolled her eyes and turned to face Aunt Vee. "Don't be silly," she admonished.

Vanessa Harrington hadn't changed one bit since the last time Clara had seen her. She was in her early seventies now, but didn't seem to have aged at all in at least a decade. She was tall, walked with purpose, and maintained a very fashionable, short hairstyle.

"I'm getting on, you know," Vanessa complained as she stepped through the gate and held her arms wide open. "Come here."

Clara did as she was instructed and hugged her aunt tightly. It had been two years since they'd seen each other, but Clara always stayed in touch via phone calls.

"You're too skinny," Vanessa complained.

Clara didn't say anything; no one could accuse Vanessa of having an ounce of fat on her frame.

"I'm happy with my weight, Aunt Vee," Clara told her.

Vanessa let her go and leaned back, looking her up and down critically before letting out a "hmm." She turned her attention to Terry. "Bring the bags in, Terence."

She took Clara's arm in hers and walked her down the pathway. Clara looked over her shoulder. "I… I don't think that's part of his job."

"Nonsense, what else is he going to do around here?" Vanessa stood to one side and gestured for her to enter.

Clara admired the heavy, black door; it was clearly an original feature of the house. The hallway had beautiful flagstone tiles, but the walls looked much newer and the ceilings weren't nearly as low as she thought they'd be.

The cottage displayed many original features in between skilful modernisation. It was light and airy, the windows all being relatively new and double-glazed. The walls were painted in light creams and were free of any of the usual lumps and bumps Clara associated with cottages of a similar age.

"It's beautiful, Aunt Vee," she said as she admired an antique bookshelf.

"Of course it is," Vanessa said. "Your room is the one up the stairs and first on the left. The bathroom is up there, second on the left, if you'd like to freshen up. I'll sort Terry out and pay his bill, and then I'll get the kettle on and we'll hear all about what's been happening with you."

Clara knew better than to argue. She wasn't being asked if she wanted to look at her room and freshen up; she was being told to do so. Vanessa wasn't asking if it would be okay for her to pay the taxi fare; she was going to. And that was that.

There was something comforting about being back with her favourite—and only—aunt. Clara placed a kiss on her aunt's cheek before turning and heading up the stairs.

"Far too skinny," she heard Vanessa mutter under her breath.

3

SANDWICHES IN THE GARDEN

Clara opened up her suitcase and selected her favourite loose T-shirt to change into. The weather was pleasant, despite it being six in the evening. She couldn't remember the last time she had been home from work so early. One of the benefits of being unemployed: she got to enjoy some of the sunshine before winter gobbled it up completely.

She pulled her long, dark blonde hair from its ponytail and tossed it around a little to let it lay in casual curls around her shoulders. She'd taken her contact lenses out and slid on her full-rimmed glasses.

She felt about as human as she was going to and was eager to get downstairs and catch up with Aunt Vee. She hurried down the stairs and into the kitchen where she could hear the sound of china softly clinking.

"Can I help with anything?"

Vanessa looked up from where she was plating sandwiches. "Goodness. You look like a French onion seller."

Clara looked down at her white top with horizontal

black stripes and rolled her eyes. "It's my favourite T-shirt, so you'll have to get used to it."

Vanessa raised her eyebrow but said nothing further. She gestured to the two trays she had stacked up on the counter, one contained plates and sandwiches, one a tea service. "Take one of these out to the garden, I thought we'd sit outside while the weather is still nice."

Clara picked up the tea service, deciding that it was probably the heavier of the two trays. She walked through the living room and towards the open patio doors that led into the back garden.

She glanced down at her aunt's writing desk as she passed, wondering what she was working on at the moment. There was a closed red leather book with a fountain pen atop it in the middle of table, and Clara's interest was piqued.

"Are you working on a book?" she asked.

"I'm always working on a book," Vanessa replied.

It was true, she'd been writing almost continuously for fifty-five years—more than double the amount of time Clara had been alive.

She decided to question her aunt about her latest writing project another time and stepped out into the garden. Like the front, the back was idyllic and well-manicured. Large bushes framed the perimeter, and a wrought-iron patio set stood in the middle of a small, paved area. Overflowing flower beds and planters were scattered around the peaceful space.

Clara decided immediately that she would be spending as much time as possible in the garden during her stay. Weather allowing, naturally.

She lowered the tray to the table and stood up. She

looked around the space in more detail. Around three hundred metres ahead, in between two bushes, she could see a very large house.

"That's Chadwick Manor," Vanessa explained as she entered the garden balancing the second tray.

Clara took the tray from her. "Looks big."

"It is. This is the old gatekeeper's cottage; their driveway runs along the side of the house and the garden." Vanessa pointed to the bushes. "I see all sorts."

Clara bet she did. Vanessa wasn't shy about spying on her neighbours. Clara would place a bet that she would be able to locate at least three pairs of binoculars inside the cottage.

"Sit down, you need to eat," Vanessa told her.

Clara chuckled to herself and took a seat. "This looks delicious, thank you."

"It's just some sandwiches, I didn't know if you'd eat on the train. Tomorrow, I'll take you to the local shop, and we can get some supplies. It's an experience, shopping for groceries here."

"I bet it is. I take it you don't have a local supermarket?" Clara asked.

"No, we have Higginbottom's, the nosiest grocer in Buckinghamshire. I sometimes order random items just to mess with him. I asked for three dish brushes the other week, and I specified they needed to be in different colours. I suspect it drives him mad not knowing what I need them for."

Clara laughed. "Oh, you are mean!"

"I am," Vanessa agreed. "But enough about me. I want to hear about you. How are you?"

"I'm good." Clara lied easily as she poured herself some tea. She couldn't remember the last time she'd poured tea from a teapot rather than consumed it from the plastic mouthpiece of a takeaway mug.

"You always were a terrible liar," Vanessa told her, an accusatory finger pointed in her niece's direction.

Clara sagged. "Fine, I'm miserable. I keep auditioning for work as a violinist, but it's so hard to get anything these days. I was a receptionist at LTC, as you know, but they went bankrupt after the chief financial officer decided to use the corporate account for his holidays."

"Odious little creep," Vanessa said.

"Yes, he was," Clara agreed. "I hated that job, but at least it paid the bills."

"And your landlord?" Vanessa asked. "What happened there?"

"He's been warning us all for ages that he planned to sell the building, but he promised he'd give us lots of warning. But, two days after I was suddenly out of work, I got a letter from his solicitor telling us we all had two weeks to get out."

"Surely that's illegal?"

"Probably," Clara said. "It wouldn't have mattered, I had to move out. But, without a job, there was no chance of me getting a new lease. Of course, let's not forget that Jenny dumped me a month before." She slumped in her chair and mumbled, "I still miss her."

"You shouldn't. You're far too good for her."

"But I still miss her," Clara argued.

"Well, stop missing her. It's wasted effort," Vanessa replied as if Clara had any such control.

Clara knew her aunt didn't mean to sound unfeeling; she

was just a very practical woman. She'd spent a lifetime writing books in which she could control every character's actions and thoughts. Now she tried to match that ability in the real world, with varied results. Sometimes her no-nonsense approach was exactly what Clara needed to hear. Sometimes it missed the mark.

"Anyway," Clara said, emphasising the word to indicate that that part of the conversation was over, "everything happened at once."

"It did. You deserve a break; you know you're welcome to stay here as long as you like."

Clara smiled. She knew Vanessa meant it. While she'd never been the most maternal of sorts, she'd always doted on her niece, and Clara had lapped up the attention. Vanessa had never had children of her own and never married, which meant she'd always had a fair amount of free time to spend with her brother's only child.

"Have you heard from your mother?" Vanessa asked.

Clara shook her head. "Not this year. I had a Christmas card last year."

"Ah, yes, I received one, too. With a photo of her new family, all looking perfect in front of an ostentatious Christmas tree. What a strange thing to send to the family you used to have and now choose to ignore."

Clara wanted to defend her mother, but she couldn't. She opened her mouth to try to stumble through an explanation of some sort, but the sound of a car passing by the garden at great speed stopped her.

Vanessa narrowed her eyes and stared at one of the bushes, obviously knowing exactly where the gaps were that allowed her to see through.

"I thought so," she said to herself.

"Hmm?" Clara asked.

"Jemima Vos, she lives next door. Well, I say next door, she lives at the farm next to the Chadwick Estate. Drives like a lunatic. The Chadwicks must be having a dinner."

"Have you ever been to dinner there?"

Vanessa laughed. "Goodness me, no. I'm not important enough to be invited up to the big house. I've seen Mrs Chadwick, Genevieve, once or twice. And they have a daughter, Pippa, she's an odd sort. Very quiet. And Angus Chadwick, don't get me started. But on the whole, we keep to ourselves."

"When I arrived at the station, the porter asked if I was a Chadwick. Looked horrified at the prospect," Clara said, remembering her interaction with the young man.

"That would be Edward Milton, he is dating Pippa Chadwick. Well, they try to. Angus doesn't like it one bit, so I hear."

"Ah, that would explain the bad blood. He wasn't happy at all when I said I was coming to Chadwick… I couldn't remember that it was the lodge." Clara picked up another sandwich. She could tell they had been made with real butter, not spread. She suspected her stay would result in some serious weight gain, which would no doubt please Vanessa greatly.

The sound of car tyres crunching over pieces of gravel sounded on the other side of the border. Vanessa raised her eyebrow.

"That's three," she said. "Julian Bridgewater arrived just before you did. Jemima, and now…" She angled her head a few times to try to get a glimpse of the latest car to make its way to Chadwick Manor. "Ah, I believe that's Felicity Abbot."

"Another neighbour?" Clara asked.

"No, she's a councillor. Works with Angus on the parish council. Well, he is the head of the council, and she does all the work."

Clara sighed. It was a story she heard time and time again. The men took the glory, the women did the work.

"Quite the party happening up there," she commented.

"Yes," Vanessa agreed. She reached for a sandwich. "How awful for them."

4

A MURDER

The sound of a creaking floorboard woke Clara up. She sat up and looked around the unfamiliar space. Confusion filled her for a few seconds until she remembered where she was.

Her old room in the house share in Lewisham was gone. She was a guest of her aunt, not for the first time in her life. When her parents had divorced, the option of staying with Vanessa had been brought up. It was supposed to be just until the dust settled. It ended up being for four years.

Even though she had never been to Chadwick Lodge, or Picklemarsh, surrounded by her aunt's familiar scent and some of the furniture and decorations of her youth, Clara somehow felt like she had come home.

She heard the creak again and peered around the bed to figure out where it was coming from. It was dark, very dark. She was used to London streetlights providing a dim glow. She picked up her phone and saw that it was just after one in the morning.

She got out of bed and pulled on the dressing gown Vanessa had lent her the night before. She'd warned that it got chilly in the mornings—another lovely effect of Pickle-marsh being in a ditch.

Clara carefully crossed the unfamiliar room and opened the door. She peeked out on the landing, wondering if they were being robbed or if Vanessa was up and about.

"Look at this."

Clara gasped and jumped. At the end of the hallway, sat on the window ledge with a pair of binoculars fixed on something in the distance, was Vanessa.

"You scared me!" Clara complained.

"Someone's dead," Vanessa said, gesturing her head towards the window.

Clara wrapped the dressing gown around her tightly and crossed the landing.

"What do you mean?"

"I mean that someone is dead," Vanessa repeated. "What do you think I mean? And the police think it's suspicious, too."

Clara leaned against the wall and looked out of the window. She could see the faint glow of blue alternating lights in the distance.

"Is that coming from Chadwick Manor?"

"Yes. The first police car arrived at twenty minutes past ten," Vanessa explained. "Ten minutes after that, an ambulance silently and slowly made its way down the drive. From that we can deduce that there was no emergency for them to rush to." She lowered her binoculars and looked meaningfully at Clara. "Presumably because the victim was already dead."

"Aunt Vee!" Clara chided. "You don't know that."

"Ten minutes later, another police car and another vehicle, presumably belonging to a detective, arrived." Vanessa raised the binoculars again and continued her appraisal of the situation. "An hour and a half later, the ambulance left. The police cars all remain. I didn't hear any of the dinner guests leave, so we can assume they are all still there. Being questioned."

Clara folded her arms across her chest to keep the chill at bay. As much as she hated to admit it, it sounded likely that her aunt was right. Why else would an ambulance spend ninety minutes at Chadwick Manor, only for the police to stay for another hour? And why had none of the dinner guests left, considering it was well after midnight?

Vanessa shifted her weight on the window ledge. It let out a small creak, and Clara realised that was what had woken her up.

"Shush," Vanessa complained to the wooden plinth beneath her. "Honestly, you'd think I was a hippopotamus the way it complains."

"Are you sure you're not jumping to conclusions?" Clara asked.

"About the party? Am I not allowed to? I've been writing crime novels longer than you've been alive," Vanessa stated.

Clara knew that her aunt would love a real murder on her doorstep. Most people would quake in fear at such an insidious crime being committed, but Vanessa Harrington had written about murder her entire working life. If she wasn't writing about it, she was reading about it, researching it, or watching TV dramas about it.

"We'll see. The police will come in the morning. We're witnesses." Vanessa grinned with glee.

"Aunt Vee, someone might be dead," Clara admonished the older woman's delight.

"We're all going to die eventually," Vanessa told her. "And, if there was a murder, then there'll be an investigation. And, if the police are any good, there'll be a conviction." She lowered her binoculars and looked at Clara kindly. "It's the way of the world. People kill each other. You know that; you've lived in London your entire life."

Clara swallowed. She knew it was true, but that didn't mean she had to like it.

"Get some rest," Vanessa told her.

"I'm not sure I'll be able to now," Clara said. "Not now that you think there's a murderer on the loose."

"Not on the loose," Vanessa said. She pointed towards Chadwick Manor. "In there."

5

INSPECTOR ELLIS

Clara was awoken by the sound of plates, pots, and pans being moved in the kitchen downstairs. A smile graced her lips as she remembered Vanessa's utter inability to be quiet in the morning. At one point in her life, Clara had grown used to being woken up by what sounded like the entire kitchen being reorganised every single morning.

Her phone told her it was seven-thirty, not a bad time to be woken up. Vanessa had probably been awake for an hour.

She got out of bed and lifted the lid of one of her suit-cases. Unpacking would be on her to-do list that day, she hadn't been able to face the prospect the night before. She picked out some clothes, a casual light sweater and some skinny jeans.

Ten minutes later she entered the kitchen, dressed and relatively presentable.

"Morning," she greeted.

"Eggs?" Vanessa asked, a frying pan in her hand.

"Morning," Clara repeated.

"Yes, yes, good morning, Clara." She rolled her eyes. "Would you like some eggs for breakfast?"

"No, thank you, I'll just have some toast." Clara opened the breadbin and pulled out the loaf of white bread, making a mental note to purchase some wholemeal later that day.

"What do you think you're doing?" Vanessa asked.

Clara put two slices of bread into the toaster, smothering a yawn behind her hand. "Making toast, would you like some?"

"*I'm* making breakfast."

"You don't have to wait on me."

"I'm not waiting on you. You're a guest, I'm the host. I make the breakfast." Vanessa put the frying pan down on the counter.

"I can make my own breakfast," Clara replied, already looking in the fridge for the butter.

"Fine, but I'm making the tea." Vanessa grabbed the kettle and took it over to the sink to fill it up. "Unless you prefer coffee?"

"Tea is fine."

There was a sharp rap on the front door. Vanessa abandoned the kettle on the counter and grinned. "Here we go!" She practically skipped to the front door.

Clara rolled her eyes. She wasn't awake enough to deal with a police investigation, or her aunt's apparent joy that someone had probably been killed. She got a butter knife out and prodded the rock-solid brick of butter.

"Spread," she muttered to herself. "Get some spread."

"This is Detective Inspector Ellis," Vanessa said as she returned to the kitchen. "Tea, Inspector?"

Clara turned to see the stocky man enter the room. He

wore a mid-priced suit; his tie was slightly askew. He was in his mid-thirties but had a baby face that Clara assumed wasn't an asset in his line of work.

"Thank you, Miss. That's very kind. Pleasure to meet you." He nodded at Clara and stood awkwardly in the doorway.

Clara held out her hand. He smiled and shook it.

"Clara Harrington," she greeted.

"Will Ellis."

Clara gestured to a chair at the round kitchen table. "Please, sit down. You'll have to excuse me; I'm just eating my breakfast." She turned her attention back to the toaster.

"I'm sorry for calling in so early. I noticed movement and assumed you were awake."

"It's quite all right, Inspector," Vanessa replied as she put the kettle on. "I'm sure you have a very good reason."

"Please, call me Will. I'm afraid I have some rather disturbing news."

"There was a murder at Chadwick Manor last night," Vanessa guessed as she pulled three cups and saucers from a shelf. "And you've yet to identify the murderer."

Clara softly shook her head. Aunt Vee did so love to show off.

"May I ask how you knew that?" Will asked, clearly taken aback by the casual attitude Vanessa displayed at the terrible news.

"So, I'm right?" Vanessa asked.

"Sorry that she's so morbid, Inspector," Clara jumped in. "She writes about murder, so she thinks that everyone is as desensitised to it as she is."

"Harrington," Will whispered. His head snapped to look at Vanessa. "You're not *Vanessa* Harrington, are you?"

"Guilty." Aunt Vee grinned like the cat that got the cream. She did so love to be recognised. Clara had once joined her on a book signing in London; the queue of readers wanting a signed copy of her latest hardback had gone out of the door. Vanessa had been in her element.

Will leaned back in his chair and stared at her with awe. "I have read every single one of your books," he stated. "Multiple times. In fact, your books are the whole reason I got into this line of work to start with."

Clara rescued her nearly cremated bread from the toaster and focused on trying to get a small amount of butter from the still rocklike brick.

She loved her aunt dearly, but she didn't look forward to the rest of the day. Aunt Vee's ego was big enough as it was without the extra input Will Ellis was providing her.

"Oh, really?" Vanessa said. "Well, how marvellous. Which is your favourite book?"

"Now that's a question! I think it would be impossible to say. Of course, I loved *Ten to Midnight*, but then I liked the twists and turns of *The Squeaky Wheel*. I thought you lived in London?"

"I did, I moved out here a couple of years ago," Vanessa explained. "I wanted to try something new. And that old house was far too big for just me. You know, my publisher always told me that *The Squeaky Wheel* was too dark, I had to fight to get that one published."

"Too dark?" Will barked a laugh. "It's no darker than, say, *Pennies in the Lake*."

"That is precisely what I said, wasn't it, Clara?"

"You did, Aunt Vee," Clara agreed. She turned around and looked at Will Ellis. "So, has there been a murder?"

Will's face turned sombre as if he suddenly remembered the reason for his visit. Clara snatched up her toast and took a seat at the kitchen table.

"Ah, yes. I'm sorry to report that Angus Chadwick was murdered last night."

"Angus?" Vanessa asked. She didn't sound upset or surprised.

"Yes. Did you know the deceased well?"

"Personally? No," Vanessa said. "I knew *of* him, and we spoke once or twice. I've seen more of his wife and daughter than I have of him."

"You're sure it was murder?" Clara asked.

"We're sure," Will confirmed. "He was poisoned. Fell face down into his dessert."

"The dessert was poisoned?" Clara gasped.

"No, he didn't actually get to eat any of the dessert, he was poisoned beforehand. Our team is working on what type of poison was used and when it was delivered to the victim." Will turned his attention back to Vanessa. "Were you aware of any visitors to the property last night?"

"Of course, the only driveway runs past my house. We deduced early on in the evening that they were having a gathering of some kind." Vanessa filled the teapot with steaming hot water from the kettle. "Of course, every one of them has a reason to want Angus dead."

"Could you elaborate on that?" Will asked.

"Isn't that your job, Inspector?" Vanessa asked. "Unless you need my help?"

Will shifted uncomfortably in his seat. "Not at all, just

asking for any information you might like to share with me as part of an ongoing investigation."

Vanessa brought the tea tray over to the table. She placed cups and saucers out for the three of them. "I'd love to collaborate with you, Inspector, but all I have to offer is hearsay and rumour, nothing that an official investigation would want to hear about."

Clara focused intently on her toast. She didn't want to get involved in the power play that was happening before her eyes. Vanessa clearly wanted to be involved in the investigation, and, if Clara knew her aunt, she would be involved one way or another.

If Will sought her help, then she'd have all the access she needed. If he didn't, well, Vanessa would do as she wanted regardless.

"Are you aware of any threats to Mr Chadwick's life? Has there been any hearsay or rumour recently?" he asked.

Vanessa poured tea into his cup. She shook her head. "It's not my experience that people announce their intention to murder someone. Especially with poison, which I would think is a premeditated action."

"Can you think of anyone who would personally gain from Mr Chadwick's death?" Will tried again. He took the proffered milk jug from Vanessa's hand and poured a little into his cup.

"Almost everyone in Picklemarsh," Vanessa said. "He was the head of the council. Who doesn't have a quarrel with the head of their local government? And he wasn't exactly well liked by his family or neighbours. I'm sorry, Inspector, it would be difficult to give you any accurate information without having some kind of access to the case."

"I'm afraid I can't do that, Miss Harrington," Will told her.

"Oh, that's a shame. I was often brought in as an advisor to Chief Inspector Ludlow. In the Met. In London."

Clara couldn't believe the boldfaced lies slipping from her aunt's lips. She stared at her over the top of her toast but was completely ignored.

Will looked flustered. "Um... well..."

"I thought you were in charge of the investigation?" Vanessa asked.

"I am," he replied quickly.

"So, it would be your decision. But I understand if you feel your masculinity would be called into question if you had us two at your side." Vanessa picked up a cube of sugar and dropped it into her cup with a splash.

"Us *two*?" Clara asked. How had she suddenly gotten involved in this?

"You know I need help, dear," Vanessa told Clara. She turned to Will. "I'm rather old, you see, Inspector. I like to have my niece with me, but my mind is still there. We wouldn't get in your way."

Clara just shook her head. The show her aunt was putting on was worthy of a BAFTA.

"I don't think it's a good idea, Miss Harrington. But thank you for offering your time, I know you must be busy," Will said, politely but firmly.

"Indeed, I am," Vanessa agreed. "I'm afraid I don't have much to say about Angus. He was disliked, as you'll find throughout the course of your investigation. Beyond that... as I say, hearsay."

Clara kept silent. She knew exactly what her aunt was

doing and suspected that Will wasn't foolish enough to fall for it either. He looked at her for a few seconds before quickly downing his tea.

He stood up and reached into his jacket pocket, then put a business card on the table.

"If you hear of anything that you think I ought to know about, please give the station a call," he said.

"Of course," Vanessa agreed. "Let me see you out, Inspector."

Clara smiled to herself. Vanessa had clearly lost this battle, but if Clara knew her aunt, then she was also pretty sure that the war was not over.

6

HIGGINBOTTOM GREENGROCER'S

"Chief Inspector Ludlow?" Clara asked with eyebrow raised the moment she saw Will step foot out of the front garden and into the street.

Vanessa returned to the kitchen. "I told you it was a murder."

"And Inspector Ellis told you not to get involved," Clara reminded her, knowing it was a pointless endeavour but feeling the need to try.

"No, Inspector Ellis insisted he didn't need our help with the official investigation. There's no reason for us to not conduct our own." Vanessa started to clear away the breakfast things.

"Our?" Clara questioned, again wondering how she had gotten roped into this.

"Let's get ready to head out. We need groceries. Maybe we could pop into the council offices; they are right next door."

Clara sighed. There was no point in arguing with Aunt Vee when she had her mind set on something, and, for some reason, she was absolutely set on investigating Angus Chadwick's murder.

Clara finished her tea and then helped to clear things away in the kitchen. When they were done, she followed Aunt Vee up the stairs. Vanessa hurried straight into her bedroom, obviously eager to get ready and get going.

Clara stood outside the bedroom door. She leaned on the wall and stared up at the ceiling.

"Why do we have to investigate this?" she asked.

"Aren't you intrigued?" her aunt asked. "There's a murderer on the loose."

"Then all the more reason to stay at home and out of people's way. Especially out of the way of people who have recently committed a murder and might be worried about being caught."

"No one is running through the streets of Picklemarsh with a chainsaw, dear. It was poison. Just… be careful what you eat."

"Is today really the best day to buy groceries?" Clara asked, half joking.

"Oh. Good point! We must find out what was being served at dinner last night," Aunt Vee said.

"And how do we do that?"

Vanessa burst through the doorway, a picture of excitement. "This is an English village, my dear. Everyone knows everything about everyone else."

Clara thought that Picklemarsh was very picturesque with its narrow, winding roads and thatched cottages. It was a gardener's paradise with beautifully kept gardens, enormous trees, and fields in any direction she looked.

Sadly, she wasn't able to enjoy much of it as Aunt Vee marched her through the short high street which comprised of less than fifteen shops. In fact, calling it a high street was most definitely overselling it.

In the middle of everything was Higginbottom Grocer's, housed in a building that looked like it hadn't changed much in three hundred years, with a shop window which looked about as old as Vanessa.

Aunt Vee was full of energy, her long legs affording her a fast stride in her quest to find more information about the events of last night.

"Follow my lead, don't say anything," she instructed Clara in a whisper as they both entered the grocer's.

Inside the store were three aisles, packed with shelves of all kinds of food and household items. Every wall contained more shelves, and at the back of the shop was a large desk covered in newspapers for sale and a till which must have been forty years old.

Behind the desk stood a stout man in his sixties. He wore a shirt and tie, his sleeves rolled up to his elbows. "Good morning, Miss Harrington," he greeted.

"Hello, Alf," Vanessa greeted as she picked up a shopping basket from the small stack by the door. "This is my niece, Clara."

Clara offered a wave. Alf gave her a nod and a smile in return.

Vanessa gestured that they should start looking at the aisles. Clara grabbed a loaf of wholemeal bread and placed it in the basket. Vanessa looked at it as if it were a loaded gun.

"What's that for?"

"Eating," Clara said. "You don't have to eat it, but it's what I prefer."

Vanessa's eyebrow raised as she stared at the loaf. "No wonder you're so thin."

"Did you hear?"

Clara jumped, though Vanessa merely turned her head to regard Alf with a curious expression.

"Hear what?"

"About Angus," Alf said, his voice a whisper as he looked around the completely empty shop.

"What about him?" Vanessa returned her attention to her shopping, picking up a carton of eggs and examining the box with a sneer.

"Dead. Murdered." Alf nodded his head. "Last night. You wouldn't have heard all the commotion; you would have been asleep, but I heard it all. I could hear a mouse moving a pebble in the night these days."

"How do you know he was murdered?" Vanessa asked, still looking disinterested in the tale of murder, thoroughly engaged in her hunt for the perfect carton of eggs.

"Anton Vos told me," Alf explained. "He was in here this morning. He was furious that the police kept Jemima until the early hours. They wouldn't let her have access to her phone, so he had no idea what was going on. When she finally got home, she was distraught."

"I see," Vanessa said. "Still, he must be pleased that this means his land dispute with Angus is now over?"

Alf sucked in a deep breath and nodded. "Well, there is that. But Anton wasn't at the dinner, he couldn't have done it."

"No, but his wife could have," Vanessa pointed out.

Alf chuckled. "Jemima wouldn't have killed Angus. Certainly not over the land dispute. If she was going to do that then she would have done it years ago. No, if you want a motive then you want to look towards her next door." He tilted his head back to indicate the building beside the shop.

"Who?" Vanessa asked, walking further along the aisle and forcing Alf to follow her if he wanted to continue gossiping.

Which he did.

"Felicity Abbot. She's wanted to be head of the council for years. With Angus gone, she automatically takes his place." Alf leant on the corner of a shelf. "I hear that she's already making changes, cementing her positing on the council."

"And you really think that Felicity Abbot would, what, strangle Angus?" Vanessa asked.

"He was poisoned," Alf said. "And before you say it, it was nothing to do with my food. It was all catered by that place up at Mead Farm, overpriced nonsense if you ask me. The only food at that dinner that came from here was the dessert, and he fell face first into it." He tutted. "Tiramisu. Such a waste."

"And how do we know he was poisoned?" Vanessa asked. She picked up and squeezed a few oranges before putting them back in the box on the shelf and moving on.

Alf eyed the oranges in confusion before hurrying after her.

"Jemima Vos said that's what the police said. Apparently, he was all well and fine, and then he just died. They thought it was a heart attack, but the police said it looked like poison."

Vanessa hummed. She turned to Clara. "You've not become a vegan, have you? I hear it's trendy."

"No, Aunt Vee," Clara replied.

"Vegetarian?"

Clara shrugged. "I'm watching the amount of meat I eat, but I'm not a vegetarian."

"I want to know why he was hosting a dinner last night," Alf continued. "Anton said that they were all invited to a meal because Angus wanted to tell them something."

"And did he?" Vanessa asked.

"I don't know," Alf admitted.

"So, either he didn't get to the reason for gathering them all there, or Jemima didn't tell Anton. Or Anton didn't tell you."

"Why would Anton not tell me?" Alf asked.

"Because you're a terrible gossip," Vanessa told him honestly.

Alf opened his mouth, seeming to want to issue a defence. He paused and then closed his mouth again. "Fair enough," he said.

Clara heard footsteps and turned to see a woman enter the shop.

"Excuse me," Alf said and hurried over to greet the newcomer.

Vanessa leaned in close. "Interesting, don't you think?"

"What?" Clara asked.

"That Angus asked them all to dinner to tell them something. Did he get to tell them his news? Was that what pushed the killer over the edge?" Vanessa mused.

Clara folded her arms. "Would the killer be carrying poison with them, just on the off chance Angus said something they didn't like?" she asked.

Vanessa looked at her with pride. "Now you're getting into it."

Clara shook her head. "I'm not getting into it, I'm just… questioning things." She knew how weak that sounded.

"I think we should go and see Felicity Abbot," Vanessa suggested. "She's a suspect, she's next door, and… I think you should meet her."

Clara took in her aunt's raised eyebrow and quirky smile. "And why might that be?"

Vanessa continued to stroll the aisle, picking up the odd item as she walked.

"Aunt Vee, why?"

"You'll see," her aunt sniffed. "We'll finish up in here, leave the shopping with Alf, and then we'll pop next door and see what else we can find out."

7

COUNCILLOR ABBOT

The cottage next door to the greengrocer's had been converted into office space. The door opened into a small hallway which held a reception desk. Behind the desk was a small waiting room that resembled a doctor's office.

"Is Councillor Abbot in?" Vanessa asked the receptionist.

"She is, do you have an appointment?"

"Do I need one?" Vanessa asked, indicating the empty waiting room with a nod of her head.

The receptionist, a thin lady whose glasses barely balanced on the end of her nose, narrowed her eyes and begrudgingly reached for the telephone on her desk. "Who should I say would like to speak with her?"

"Vanessa Harrington."

Clara looked around as the receptionist dialled the requisite number. Various awards, certificates, and newspaper articles hung in the small reception. She zeroed in on a picture of Angus Chadwick. It was the first picture she'd seen of the man, and it sent a chill through her to realise that he was now dead.

Murdered, even.

He was in his late sixties or early seventies with a very severe look about him. His grey hair was thick and swept back; his wireframed glasses made his eyes appear beadier than they probably were. His expression was very cold, and there was no hint of a smile as he cut a ribbon to open a community centre.

Clara didn't want to judge the man based upon one photograph, but she couldn't help but feel that he probably had a few enemies around the sleepy village of Picklemarsh. He didn't look approachable, or at all friendly.

"Come on, Clara."

She turned and saw Aunt Vee already climbing the stairs. Obviously, Felicity Abbot had agreed to the see them. She hurried after her aunt, and they ascended the narrow staircase.

On the landing, there were five doors. The one right in front of the stairs had a brass nameplate that said, 'Head Councillor Angus Chadwick'.

The door was closed. Vanessa stood in front of it with a look of irritation. Clara suspected that she would like nothing more than to explore the room.

One of the other doors opened.

"Hello, Miss Harrington," a voice called. "Do come in."

"Thank you, and, please, call me Vanessa."

Clara tore her eyes away from the closed office door of Angus Chadwick and turned to greet Felicity Abbot. When her eyes landed on the councillor, she stopped dead in her tracks.

Felicity was around forty, with shoulder-length, dark hair and matching eyes. She wore a black pencil skirt and matching jacket. Clara swallowed thickly; Felicity Abbot was just her type of woman. Aunt Vee must have known that by the way she smirked lightly at her.

"This is my niece, Clara," Vanessa said. "She's staying with me for a while."

Felicity jutted out her hand. "Nice to meet you."

Clara blinked and stepped forward. She shook Felicity's hand. "Thank you, likewise."

"Please, come in. I'm afraid I don't have much time." Felicity walked into her office and gestured to the chairs in front of her desk. "Can I get you a drink? Tea, coffee, water?"

"I'll have a glass of water," Vanessa said. "Clara?"

Clara nodded, keeping her eyes down. "Yes, um. Water is fine, thank you."

Vanessa sat down, and Clara quickly sat next to her, trying to not gawk at Felicity. She would be having words with Vanessa later for not warning her about the attractive councillor.

"We heard about Angus," Vanessa said.

Clara looked up to see Felicity pouring two glasses of water from a small drinks station in the corner of her office.

"Yes, it's terrible," she replied, though she sounded preoccupied. She carried the glasses over to the desk and placed them in front of Vanessa and Clara and then sat down.

"You were at the dinner last night?" Vanessa asked, her eyes glancing down at the desk and the paperwork on top of it.

"I was." Felicity closed the file she had been working on and then interlaced her fingers, resting her hands on top.

Vanessa reached for the glass of water, but just before she was able to pick it up Felicity grabbed it. She looked at it and sighed.

"I'm sorry, this glass has a hairline crack. Let me get you another one." She was on her feet and heading back to the cabinet to replace the glass. "I don't know when that happened. I do apologise."

"It's fine," Vanessa replied. "I have quite a few in my cupboard at home that need replacing."

Felicity shivered. "I can't stand chipped glass." She got a replacement glass of water and placed it in from of Vanessa. She eyed Clara's glass to check that one was whole before retaking her seat.

"Anyway, as I was saying, is this about council business, Miss Harrington?"

"Doesn't the head of the council being murdered constitute council business?" Vanessa asked.

"There's an ongoing police investigation, so you'll understand that I can't say anything. If that's why you're here, then I'm afraid you've wasted your time. Was there anything else?" Felicity picked up a folder and a pen from her desk, obviously eager to get back to work.

"You don't seem particularly sad that the man you worked with for many, many years was murdered last night," Vanessa observed. "Right in front of you."

Clara wanted a hole to open up and swallow her. She couldn't believe that her aunt was being so blunt with her questioning. Questions she had no legal right to ask.

Felicity shrugged her shoulder. "It's no secret that we rarely saw eye to eye."

"Did you disagree with him enough to kill him?" Vanessa asked.

Felicity fixed her gaze on Vanessa. "If I had any intention of killing Angus, I would have done it many years ago."

The two women silently regarded each other for a few tense moments. Eventually, Vanessa broke the stalemate by looking around the office.

"I presume the law states that you take Angus' place in events such as these," she mused.

"It does," Felicity agreed. "Which, as I'm sure you can imagine, means that I'm very busy."

"So I see."

"We should go," Clara said. She jumped up to her feet, eager to escape the uncomfortable environment. "Sorry for wasting your time."

Felicity looked at her for a couple of seconds before offering a trace of a smile as she inclined her head. "Not at all. I hope you enjoy your time in Picklemarsh—Clara, was it?"

Clara nodded.

"I'm helping the police with their investigation," Vanessa said as she stood. "We may be back in touch."

"In which case, I'll do my best to squeeze you in," Felicity said.

"Very kind." Vanessa turned and left the office.

Clara had to hurry to follow her. All the way down the stairs she had to wonder why on earth she had let her aunt drag her into this ridiculous investigation—not to mention if she were breaking the law by pretending to be a part of an ongoing murder enquiry.

"Helping the police?" she asked as they exited the

council offices.

"I am. They just don't know it yet." Vanessa grinned. "Don't be grouchy just because you like Felicity Abbot."

Clara gasped. "I don't like her!"

Vanessa regarded her for second. "You do. She reminds me of your English teacher, Mrs Peters. You were head over heels for that woman."

"Aunt Vee!" Clara could feel the blush touching her cheeks.

"And then your violin tutor, what was her name?"

"Miss Maynard." Clara shook her head. "We're not talking about this."

"Why ever not? Miss Abbot's your type. She might be a murderer, though, I haven't decided yet, so maybe don't eat anything she offers you." Vanessa turned on her heel and walked back towards the grocer's.

"Haven't decided yet? This isn't one of your books, you know," Clara complained. "You don't get to *decide*."

They walked into Higginbottom's, and Alf lifted their previously purchased shopping bags up onto the counter.

"Did she do it?" he asked, tilting his head towards the wall his shop shared with the councillor.

"Maybe," Vanessa said. She took the bags.

"She has a motive," Alf said.

"That she does. But then, so do you," Vanessa told him.

"Me?!" Alf blanched.

"Didn't Angus turn down your request to put up a new shop sign? And only six months ago you were denied planning permission to extend out the back." Vanessa gave him the once-over. "Yes, there's plenty of motives going around. You mark my words."

8

ANOTHER DINNER GUEST

As they were putting the shopping away, Vanessa looked like she was a hundred miles away. Several times she took things out of a shopping bag and moved them from one counter to another without actually putting them away.

Clara rolled her eyes. She'd seen this before, but it was normally when her aunt was deep in research for a book.

"You can't go around telling people you're helping the police, you know," Clara told her.

"I can," Vanessa argued. "I can say whatever I like."

"Impersonating the police is against the law." Clara snatched up the tub of spread and put it in the fridge.

"I'm not impersonating anyone. Am I dressed as a police officer? No. Do I introduce myself as Inspector Harrington? No. Inspector Ellis sat at that table, my kitchen table, and asked me to get back to him if I had any information that may be pertinent to this murder enquiry. I'm just seeing what information I can discover which may assist."

Clara stared at her. "Oh, come on. You know that wasn't what he meant."

"I think we need to go and see Julian." Vanessa picked up the kettle and started to fill it, ignoring her niece's comment entirely.

Clara frowned. The name sounded familiar, but she couldn't quite place it.

Vanessa saw her confusion and sighed. "You need to work on your memory, Clara."

"I've not even been here twenty-four hours, and you're throwing all these names at me," Clara complained. She took the overflowing kettle out of Vanessa's hand and emptied a third of the pot back into the sink.

"Julian Bridgewater, he's an accountant," Vanessa explained. "If Angus had a dinner where he'd invited his wife, daughter, work colleague, accountant, and neighbour... it probably had something to do with money."

"Unless he was friends with them all?" Clara asked, putting the kettle on to boil and picking up some cups from the draining board.

"Angus didn't have friends."

"Someone must have liked him?"

Vanessa shook her head. "Not to my knowledge. His daughter has been at odds with him for a while, and his wife was having an affair."

"He sounds horrible," Clara admitted.

"He was. That's presumably why someone did him in."

"Aunt Vee," Clara reprimanded.

"What? Aren't we allowed to speak ill of the dead?" Vanessa asked with a chuckle. "I think we'll make an appointment to see Julian. You can tell him about your inheritance."

"What inheritance?"

"The one we'll make up to get you an appointment with an accountant, of course. If you could get all teary at one point and ask for a glass of water, I could have a look—"

"Absolutely not, I'm not going to lie!" Clara shook her head and leaned back against the counter in defiance.

"Not even a little fib?" Vanessa asked, a pout forming on her face.

"No, it's wrong."

"I don't know where I went wrong when I raised you," Vanessa complained, though her soft smile took the edge off the words. She softly shouldered Clara out of the way and took over the tea-making duties.

Clara was going to argue that Vanessa hadn't technically raised her but knew that was pointless. So was pointing out that Vanessa had demanded honesty back then. Clara knew that Vanessa appreciated Clara's inability to lie, she just liked to tease her about it.

"Well, we will just have to go and see Julian about my investments instead," Vanessa said.

"Do you have investments?" Clara asked, not sure if the visit would just be centred on a different lie.

"Yes. It was going to be a nice surprise for you when I died."

Clara shuddered. "Don't say things like that."

Vanessa reached out and squeezed Clara's hand, knowing that Clara hated to think about a time when Vanessa would no longer be in her life. Even if that time was ticking closer and closer.

"I'll call him after lunch and make an appointment to see him. Hopefully we can get in today."

"So, you don't really think Felicity Abbot did it?" Clara asked.

"Do you think she did?"

Clara pushed away from the counter and took a seat at the kitchen table. "I don't think I know how anyone could murder someone else."

"But do you think that Felicity Abbot could do it?" her aunt pressed.

Clara rested her head in the palm of her hand and thought about it. She didn't want to think that anyone could do that, and especially didn't want to think of Felicity as a cold-blooded poisoner. Especially as she found her insanely attractive, not that she was about to admit that to Aunt Vee.

"She has a motive," she admitted. "You said that she's wanted Angus' job for years, and she wasn't exactly distraught about his death. She even said she would have killed him years ago... so, yes, I suppose she could have done it."

She heard the garden gate opening and turned around. A well-dressed woman in her fifties, clutching a tissue and dabbing at her eyes, walked up the path.

"We have a visitor," Clara said.

Vanessa smiled. "I was rather hoping we would have one eventually."

The doorbell sounded, and Vanessa gestured for Clara to go and answer it. "Bring them through," she requested.

Clara stood up and went to the hallway, checking her appearance in the mirror by the front door before she opened it.

The woman looked slightly startled.

"Oh, hello. I'm Genevieve Chadwick. Is Vanessa in?"

Clara immediately recognised Genevieve as the name of Angus' wife.

"She is." She stood back, opened the door, and gestured for Genevieve to enter the house. "I'm Clara, Vanessa's niece."

Genevieve stepped inside; she dabbed her nose with the tissue. "Ah, I see. I presume you have both heard what's happened?"

"We have, I'm so sorry for your loss," Clara said.

"Thank you, dear."

Clara closed the front door and indicated for Genevieve to go into the kitchen.

"Genevieve, I'm so sorry to hear about poor Angus!" Vanessa said the moment she saw her.

"Thank you. It has been quite the shock."

"I bet it has. Please sit down, we were just about to have some tea. Would you like a cup?"

"Thank you, but no," Genevieve said. "I just wanted to come down and make sure you knew what happened last night and warn you that the police will probably come and ask you if you saw anything. Which I'm sure you didn't, but they have their funny little procedures to follow."

"Indeed they do. Inspector Ellis came to see us this morning. I'm afraid we were no help at all," Vanessa said. "Do they have any idea what happened?"

Genevieve studied the glass-doored cabinet where the wine glasses were kept. "They seem to think he was poisoned. I told them that he wasn't the healthiest man in the village. He liked to drink, and he was overweight. I've always said he was a candidate for a heart attack or something of that sort. Do you know, he used to eat large wedges of cheese straight from the cheese dish in the fridge of an evening?"

She turned her attention back to Vanessa. "I'm sure they will find that their initial report was wrong, and he died of natural causes. But, until they do, we all seem to be under investigation."

"All?" Vanessa asked. "Were you having a dinner party?"

"Of sorts. Angus had some announcement he wanted to make. It was myself, Pippa, Felicity Abbot, Jemima from next door, Julian Bridgewater, and Sylvester King."

Clara raised an eyebrow. They hadn't heard about Sylvester King being at the manor the night before. No doubt he'd be instantly added to her aunt's list of suspects.

"What was the announcement?" Vanessa asked.

Genevieve chuckled. "Oh, it was nonsense. He'd been speaking with a big supermarket chain and they wanted to open a store on the edge of the village, but there is another site over in Downsmead. They haven't decided between us and them yet. Angus had a plan to make sure that we got the store and the investment. Or, he thought he did, anyway. I don't actually know. He didn't make an announcement as such, just told me it was about the supermarket deal."

Clara couldn't help but think that Picklemarsh could really do with a large supermarket nearby. Sure, Alf would lose some business, but then, Alf was a big busybody. And his fruit and vegetable selection were appalling.

"Pippa must be heartbroken," Vanessa said.

Genevieve nodded. "She's in shock, I think. Trying to carry on as if nothing has happened. She's still so young."

"Twenty-four, isn't she?" Vanessa queried.

"Yes, still my baby."

Clara blinked. She was twenty-six and had considered herself very much an adult for years. Of course, she knew that people aged at different rates depending on their upbringing, but by most standards mid-twenties was adulthood. She couldn't help but wonder if Pippa Chadwick was particularly immature, or if her mother simply saw her that way.

"Anyway, I won't stay for long," Genevieve said. "I'm just doing the rounds to make sure people know the truth. Ensure that the gossip doesn't get too out of hand."

"If it's any consolation, I've not heard any gossip," Vanessa lied, obviously deciding to not mention Alf's endless commentary from earlier.

"Well, that's some good news at least." Genevieve dabbed at the corner of her eye with her tissue. "I'd best be going."

Clara gestured to the front door. "I'll see you out."

"Oh, thank you. You are kind, dear."

"If you need anything, you know where we are," Vanessa offered.

"Thank you, both of you," Genevieve said.

Clara saw the woman out of the cottage and returned to the kitchen. "How can a twenty-four-year-old be a baby?" she wondered.

Vanessa chuckled as she finished up making the tea. "When she's not allowed to grow up. Interesting that Pippa is supposedly carrying on as if nothing had happened. Not usual behaviour when your father has been murdered in your own home."

"And who did Genevieve think she was kidding with that tissue?" Clara asked. "It was bone dry, and she kept patting it over her face even though it's obvious she's not been crying at all."

"I noticed that, too, almost as if it was a prop." Vanessa placed two cups down on the kitchen table.

"Who's Sylvester King?" Clara asked.

Vanessa let out a sigh. "A terrible bore. He's a local historian, likes to consider himself an author. Very full of himself."

Clara frowned. "Why would Angus want him at a dinner to discuss a supermarket?"

"No idea."

"And the neighbour, what was her name?"

"Jemima Vos," Vanessa supplied. "She owns some fields down by Marsh Lane—maybe the supermarket is considering that location? If she is the landowner, Felicity is the councillor who would approve the plans, Julian is an accountant who might be involved... that would all make sense."

"But not the local historian," Clara pointed out.

"Not the local historian," Vanessa agreed.

"I think we should go and speak to him," Clara suggested, in spite of herself.

Vanessa slumped in her chair. "Oh, must we?"

"I thought you'd be pleased! I'm enabling your ridiculous desire to investigate this case," Clara said. "Is he that bad?"

"Yes," Vanessa replied bluntly.

Clara sipped her tea. She'd dig more into why her aunt disliked Sylvester King so much later. "Okay, so, you still want to see the accountant? What's his name, Julian?"

Vanessa narrowed her eyes. "You're suddenly keen?"

Clara sat back in the chair and held the cup in the palm

of her hand, enjoying the warmth radiating through the china. "It looks like it's going to be unavoidable. The widow came to your door twelve hours after her husband was murdered. The one and only greengrocer in the village pounced on you the second you stepped inside the store. The police were here first thing. And, if you're going to tell the local councillor that you're assisting them, no doubt Inspector Ellis will be back. Might as well embrace it."

A grin spread across Vanessa's face, like the cat that got the cream.

"That's the spirit."

9

THE ACCOUNTANT

Clara held the rear car door open and waited for Vanessa to climb out. Once she was out, Clara shouted a thank you in to Terry and slammed the door closed.

"Why do they call him Big Dave?" she wondered.

"Because the previous taxi driver around here was a large man called Dave," Vanessa explained. "He sold his taxi business to Terence, but the name stuck."

Clara didn't think that made much sense, but she also knew she wouldn't get a better reason than that. She was going to have to get used to Picklemarsh and its odd ways.

"Come on, we don't want to miss our appointment." Aunt Vee nodded towards the grand-looking, modern building which contained Julian Bridgewater's accountancy offices.

"Is this all his?" Clara marvelled at the three-story building which was located on the edge of the village.

"He rents a floor out to a film company, but the rest is for him and his employees. He's known around here to be the person to go to for all financial needs—investments, mortgages, pensions, the lot."

"Does he manage your finances?" Clara asked.

"Of course not, he's a crook." Vanessa sniffed haughtily.

She walked towards the front door, and Clara quickly fell into step behind her. They walked through the automatic doors and approached the fancy reception desk which housed not one but two receptionists.

"Vanessa Harrington for Julian," Vanessa greeted one of them.

"Thank you, Miss Harrington. If you'd like to take a seat, I'll let him know that you're here."

Vanessa and Clara walked over to a cluster of leather sofas and sat down. Vanessa leaned forward and rifled through the magazines on the coffee table. She picked up a copy of a woman's magazine and leafed through it.

"Pick up a newspaper, Clara," she instructed her niece. "Quickly now."

Clara grabbed a copy of the local newspaper, opened it up, and started to read about a vegetable-growing contest. She was about to ask why she was being ordered to cover her hands with newsprint when she heard a familiar voice.

Felicity Abbot.

Clara sat as still as stone but lowered the edge of her newspaper and looked out the corner of her eye. Felicity was speaking to a tall man in his fifties. He wore a smart suit and had a slimy grin that Clara instantly took a dislike to.

She couldn't hear what they were saying, so she just watched them, idly wondering what it was about Felicity that she liked. She'd always had a thing for older women, since she first knew she was gay, but they also frightened her a little, which made dating extremely problematic.

Felicity turned around, and Clara focused her attention back on the newspaper, hoping that they weren't about to be spotted. Luck was on their side. Felicity left, seemingly without noticing them.

The man she was talking to walked into the waiting room.

"Hello, Vanessa," he said. "Lovely to see you."

Vanessa lowered her magazine. "Hello, Julian. This is my niece, Clara."

Julian turned to her and inclined his head in greeting. Now that he was up close, Clara disliked him even more. His face was extremely angular, his eyes were very close together, and his smile was snake-like.

"Hello," she said softly.

"I am so sorry to bother you today of all days," Aunt Vee began, "but Clara needs some financial advice and she's not in town for very long before she has to get back to London."

Clara slowly turned to regard her aunt, hoping that her stare conveyed enough anger to let Aunt Vee know that she would be getting some serious silent treatment when they got home.

"You better come through then," Julian said, a large smile on his face.

They followed him through reception, into a corridor, and finally into a large corner office. The entire way, Clara stared daggers into Vanessa's back.

"Here we are, ladies. Please, take a seat." Julian pulled out two chairs from the four that sat around a circular meeting table by the window.

Vanessa took a seat, placing her handbag on the floor beside her. Clara noticed her glance up at the pictures and certificates on the wall before turning to face Julian. "Before we begin, I'm so sorry to hear about Angus," Vanessa said.

Julian slowly nodded. "It's a terrible thing, a great loss."

"Very true," Vanessa agreed. "And poison, the poor man. I do hope he didn't suffer?"

Julian leaned back in his chair. "He didn't seem to. One minute he was talking, the next he just slumped forward. Of course, I tried my best to offer some medical support, but my army days are long gone. And, to be honest, I only knew the basics at best back then."

"Well, thank goodness you were there," Vanessa said, piling it on thick. Clara had to do her best to stop her eyes from exploring the tops of her eyelids.

"I just wish we could have stopped whoever did it," Julian said.

"Do you really think it was someone who knew him?" Vanessa asked. "Surely it was a table of his nearest and dearest? Seems a bit farfetched that one of them would want to murder him."

"It's not common knowledge, but his wife was having an affair," Julian explained. "And Felicity Abbot has been trying to get his job for years. Sylvester King, well, I don't know what was going on there, but he had some kind of power over Angus."

"Power?" Vanessa enquired.

"Yes. Angus was loath to talk about it, but something had changed in their relationship over the past few months." Julian shrugged.

"Wasn't Jemima Vos also present? I recall hearing her car

last night," Vanessa said. "You know how she drives like a woman possessed."

"She was there," Julian said. "Which was a surprise. I know she is a friend of Genevieve's, but Angus swore to have nothing to do with Anton or Jemima when the land dispute started up. I suppose she had reason to want him dead; then Anton will stop going on and on about the fence."

"Is that what the dispute was about? A fence?" Vanessa asked.

"Yes, there was a storm four years ago, and a fence came down. Angus had his men put it back up, but Anton says that they put it up in the wrong place. Two metres onto his land."

Clara couldn't help but get involved. "They've been arguing for four years over two metres of fence?"

Julian smiled. "Yes, they are both very headstrong. They haven't spoken in person for about a year. Which obviously makes it hard for Genevieve and Jemima, as they are friends."

"Who do you think killed him?" Vanessa asked bluntly.

Julian didn't seem at all taken aback by her question. Instead he thoughtfully sucked in his cheek. "Well, if I had to name a name…" He paused. "I'd say Edward Milton."

"Was he there last night?" Vanessa asked.

"Not in plain sight, no. But it's common knowledge that he sneaks into the house to see Pippa, and no one hated Angus more than Edward. I'm sure Edward felt that Angus was the only person standing between him and true love, you know how youngsters are." He glanced at Clara. "No offence."

Clara did her best to not roll her eyes. A difficulty she was experiencing more and more frequently.

"Did you tell your suspicions to the police?" Vanessa asked.

"I did." He sat forward, indicating that he was becoming frustrated with the line of questioning. "But that's not why you're here."

"Of course not," Vanessa agreed. "You see, Clara here has come into an inheritance recently."

"Oh, I see." Julian turned to her and smiled that viper-like grin.

"Yes, a dear old aunt of mine," Clara explained. "Died suddenly in her sleep."

"On her mother's side," Vanessa added.

10

NOT A PART OF THE INVESTIGATION

"I cannot believe you did that," Clara complained. "Just dropping me in that situation and making me come up with a lie on the spur of the moment."

"But you did it, and very well, I must say."

Vanessa sat at her writing desk, making copious notes about their meeting with Julian. Clara was curled up on the sofa, a mug of coffee in her grip, trying to forget about the stress. She'd fumbled her way through some sort of lie that seemed plausible.

"You mustn't do that again," Clara stated.

Her aunt simply hummed.

"I mean it."

"You saw Edward Milton at the train station when you arrived, did you not?" Vanessa turned in her chair to give Clara an inquisitive glance.

Clara had half a mind to not reply, to leave her stewing, but she knew it wouldn't help. Aunt Vee would be like a dog with a bone until she answered.

"Yes, he helped me with Charity, and my cases. He

called me a taxi, too." Clara turned towards the window. The weather was nice, and she wondered if a bike ride around the village would help calm her.

"Interesting," Vanessa said.

Clara heard her turn around and scratch at her notebook with her fountain pen.

"I might go out for a ride," Clara commented.

"Perhaps you could go near the train station and question Mr Milton?" Vanessa suggested.

Clara looked at her aunt's back and let out a long and heartfelt sigh. "I'll do no such thing. I've had enough of being an investigator for one day."

There was a loud rap on the door.

"I'll get it." Clara jumped up and went to the hallway. She opened the door and smiled. "Good afternoon, Inspector Ellis. Come in."

The inspector didn't look pleased, but Clara suspected that he was far more annoyed with Vanessa than he was with her. Either way, Clara intended to stay out of his way.

"She's through there," she said, pointing into the living room.

"Inspector, what a lovely surprise," Vanessa said, turning in her chair to smile at him.

"Miss Harrington, I've just spoken to Miss Abbot. She informs me that you told her you were part of the police investigation?" Will Ellis said, standing in the doorway and looking down at her with a firm stare.

"Did she?" Vanessa pulled off her glasses and placed them on the desk. "How extraordinary of her. I wonder why she did that."

Clara couldn't believe Aunt Vee's audacity. She wondered

if she'd always been this bad and Clara had forgotten over the passage of time, or if she had gotten worse with age.

"Interesting that Angus was blackmailing everyone over the opening of the supermarket, though, isn't it, Inspector?" Vanessa turned back to her notebook and slid her glasses back on.

Will looked at Clara inquisitively. She shrugged in response.

"Blackmail?" he asked.

"Yes, Julian Bridgewater is connected to Lawrence Lycett, who is the owner of Core Foods Limited, who own the supermarket chain that want to build a store in the village. There's a picture of them together in his office. I'm sure you saw it yourself, Inspector. From that, I would surmise that Julian invests money in Core Foods, and presumably has something to gain from a new store opening."

Vanessa closed her notebook and put the lid back on her fountain pen. "Julian wouldn't care if it opened here, in Downsmead, or on the moon. But he would care about delays caused by red tape in the council office. He'd probably care enough to lean on his good friend, and client, Angus, to make the planning permission go as smoothly as possible. In turn, Angus would want to, shall we say, leverage that desire."

Will reached into his jacket pocket, pulled out a small notepad and pen, and started to make notes.

"Angus Chadwick may have been the head of the council," Vanessa continued, "but Felicity Abbot did all the work. If he wanted to rush through any planning permission, he'd need her to do it for him. I don't think Angus would know how to operate a computer himself, so he would absolutely need Felicity onside. But Felicity would also be in the line of fire for the many residents in Picklemarsh who wouldn't want a large supermarket spoiling the area. No one would want to argue with Angus, but everyone would be quite all right arguing with Felicity."

She stood up and tucked her chair under her desk.

"Then, of course, there's Jemima Vos. She owns the land that the supermarket is likely to be built on. People think that it's her husband Anton's land, but it isn't. When the land dispute started over the fence, Anton put large swaths of their land into his wife's name. He knew Angus would come after him, and he was worried that he'd lose everything. Anton is a very paranoid man. But would Jemima Vos want to sell her land to the supermarket? Probably not."

She turned and looked at Will. "Blackmail, Inspector. I'm sure you'll agree."

Will scratched at his face as he looked at his hastily jotted notes. "Well, I'll admit that it certainly sounds like it could be, Miss Harrington."

"And this is what I found out in an afternoon, just from going about my own business. Can you imagine what I'd be able to tell you if I were part of the investigation?"

Will shook his head. "I'm sorry, Miss Harrington. I can't just let you into a murder investigation."

She shrugged. "That's quite all right. I didn't expect you to. But you can't expect me to stay inside my house and not speak to a single soul until you've cracked the case, surely? I am allowed to leave, am I not?"

"Of course, you just can't go telling people that you're a part of the investigation," Will told her.

"Who said that?" Vanessa asked.

Will blinked. "Miss Abbot…"

"Why ever did she say that? How extraordinary of her." Vanessa turned and opened the back door to the garden. "Are you staying for dinner, Inspector?"

Will looked at Clara and raised an eyebrow.

"Don't look at me," she said. She turned to Vanessa. "I'm off out for that ride. I have my phone if you need me."

"Okay, dear, be safe."

"Thank you for the offer, Miss Harrington, but I really need to get back to the station," Will said.

"I'll walk you out," Clara offered.

She grabbed her light jacket, small leather rucksack, and checked she had her keys and her phone. She stepped into the front garden with Will and closed the door behind them.

"I don't mean to be rude but is your aunt all there?" he asked.

"Don't be fooled, she's all there," Clara warned him.

"Am I being played?" A grin formed on his face.

"We're all always being played," she said. She slid her jacket on and strapped her rucksack on her back. "You'd do well to let her in on your investigation. As much as it pains me to admit it, she is very good at these kinds of things. Despite her methods."

"I can't just let anyone stroll around a murder investigation," Will said.

"Why not? She's not asking to see the body, or anything questionable like that. She just wants to know what you know, so she can put it together with what she knows. She has been working out these plots for a few years, you know."

"I know," he admitted.

Clara pulled her bike away from the wall and wheeled it towards the gate. "She'll do what she wants anyway," she said. "You might as well let her."

Will looked back towards the house thoughtfully. He scrunched up his face and let out a sigh. "We'll see."

"Great, is there anything else? I wanted to get a quick ride in before dinner. Unless you have anything else?"

Will shook his head and gestured to the road in front of the cottage.

"Thank you, Inspector." Clara nodded a farewell and pushed away on her bike.

"Call me Will!" He called after her.

11

MEETING MR KING

Clara panted for breath. It felt good to exhaust herself on a ride through the village streets and the surrounding country-side. Picklemarsh really was picturesque, even if it had just been the location of a murder.

As much as she tried to push it out of her mind, she couldn't. Someone had poisoned Angus Chadwick. That person had very likely been at dinner with him, and, so far, everyone had a very good motive for wanting him dead.

It felt surreal to be looking at people and wondering if they'd committed such a crime, but she couldn't shake it. As the wind blew through her hair, she found herself wondering who had done it.

Was it Genevieve, the wife who everyone seemed to think was having an affair, the one who clutched a bone-dry tissue to dry her fake tears? Was it Julian, who apparently had a financial incentive? Or Felicity, who had finally achieved her lifelong career goals through the unexpected death of her boss?

Then there were Anton and Jemima Vos, whom she'd yet

to meet. And Pippa Chadwick. Could anyone really kill their own father? Clara supposed they could under the right circumstances.

She turned a corner and found herself back in the small high street. It was like something out of the early-to-mid 1900s. A baker, a butcher, a greengrocer. The supermarket would certainly shake things up if it did ever get built.

Towards the end of the row of shops she saw Milton Furnishings and remembered Edward Milton's comment about his upcycled furniture the day before, at the train station. She stopped outside the store and looked in through the large windows. It was a small space and crammed full of dated furniture.

She wondered if she should go inside and look around, even though she was very clearly not interested in purchasing any furniture. She could pretend, she supposed. She bit her lip. Vanessa was getting into her head.

The door opened. An older man dressed in a very smart suit—complete with a cane, of all things—stepped out of the shop. He was immaculately presented and seemed fully aware of it.

A woman followed him out of the shop. She was in her forties and looked like she worked there.

"Tom can drop it off tomorrow at three, if that's convenient?" she asked.

"I will be out of the house until three-thirty," the man replied curtly, his nose in the air.

"I'll ask Tom to drop by then." The woman looked up at Clara and smiled warmly. "Can I help you?"

"I was just passing," Clara said. "I spoke with Edward yesterday, he talked about his upcycled furniture?"

"Feel free to come in and have a look around. Edward's work is just to the left as you come in." She turned back to the snobbish man. "I'll see you again soon, Mr King."

The name struck Clara as soon as it was uttered. She wondered if this was Sylvester King, a man on their list of suspects but someone Vanessa seemed to want to avoid. She'd said he was a terrible bore, a local historian and author. Clara looked at the man who was now looking at her bike with fascination. It certainly could be the same man.

"Is that an Ulster Tourist?" Mr King asked.

"It is," she confirmed.

"It's been many years since I saw one of them. It must be twice or even three times as old as you," he said, walking around the bike and taking it all in.

Clara felt uncomfortable with the level of scrutiny. It was as if she had no way to escape his intense stare. The woman from the shop decided she'd been dismissed and quickly made her exit back into the store.

"Do you like bikes?" Clara asked, trying to get Mr King to look at her rather than her legs.

"I like anything original," he replied. He stood up straight. "I'm Sylvester King." He said it as if he assumed that she would know him. Which she did, but she felt a petty urge to not let him know that.

"I'm Clara Harrington," she replied.

His eyes widened, and a smile curled at the edges of his mouth.

"Don't tell me you're related to Vanessa Harrington?"

"I'm her niece. I'm staying here for a while." Clara looked up and down the street, hoping that someone, anyone, would be passing so she would no longer be the sole focus of Sylvester's attention. There was something about him that she didn't like.

"I see good looks run in the family," he said, presumably thinking he was charming as he said so.

Clara swallowed and tried to smile. "Thank you," she murmured.

"I was intending to pop over and see dear Vanessa in the next couple of days. I'm sure she's spoken about me?" His gaze returned to her bike or, more specifically, her legs.

"I've... only been in town a little while," Clara said. She shifted uncomfortably.

"Hello again!"

Clara turned and saw Edward Milton walking towards her. She'd never been so happy to see someone in her life.

"Hi, Edward," she greeted him.

Edward smiled at her and then turned to Sylvester. "Hi, Mr King. I think I saw that police officer knocking on your door a couple of minutes ago."

Sylvester rolled his eyes. "Useless plods, I've told them everything I know. Including the *identity* of the murderer."

Clara looked at him in askance. He smiled smugly.

"Who do you think did it?" she finally questioned, realising that he was waiting to be asked.

"It's rather obvious, I don't know how no one else has seen it." He remained silent, obviously waiting for someone to beg him to explain all.

"Well, I only just got here," Clara pointed out.

"Look no further, Miss." Sylvester looked over her shoulder. "Speak the devil's name, and she shall appear."

Clara turned. Felicity Abbot was walking out of the council offices holding her briefcase, coat over her arm. She looked like she was heading home for the day, which reminded Clara that time was getting on and she should probably get back to Vanessa soon.

"So, to clarify," Clara asked, turning back to Sylvester. "You're saying that Felicity Abbot murdered Angus Chadwick?"

He nodded.

"And why is that so obvious?"

He looked at her and shook his head. "You'll figure it out, eventually."

Without another word, he turned and walked away. Clara wanted to call out after him, but she also didn't want to give him the satisfaction.

"Just ignore him," Edward advised.

"I'd like to, but he makes it hard." She turned and looked for Felicity, but the councillor was already gone. "Do you know why he thinks she did it?"

Edward shrugged. "Who knows what goes on inside his head."

"I'm sorry to hear about your girlfriend's dad, by the way," Clara said, realising that she hadn't acknowledged the fact that Edward, or Pippa, for that matter, were probably grieving a loss.

He shrugged again. "We didn't see eye to eye. He was vile to Pippa."

"Still, he was her dad," Clara said.

"Yeah, but she's had years of him being awful. I think she's just relieved right now." Edward's eyes widened as he realised what he'd said. "I mean, she didn't kill him or anything like that, but she's not exactly going to miss him."

Clara briefly wondered if Edward would kill for Pippa.

"Who do you think did it?"

Edward laughed. "Honestly? Could be any of them. He wasn't a very well-liked man."

"But you don't have any inkling?"

He folded his arms and leaned against a lamppost as he considered the question. "He made Anton's life a nightmare with this land dispute. But then Anton wasn't at the dinner, unless he somehow poisoned him beforehand? But I heard from Alf that the police think the poison was ingested that evening, during the dinner."

Clara blinked. That was new information. But it had come from Alf, she corrected herself; she wasn't sure how accurate that was.

"Maybe Jemima?" Edward continued. "She's a bit crazy. Angus was in a legal battle with her husband, and her best friend is Genevieve, who's been miserable in her marriage for years. She's been having an affair."

"Do you know who with?" Clara asked, eager to get some more details on the supposed affair.

"Roger Smythe, from Downsmead. It's been going on for years."

"And everyone knows?" Clara asked, curious that so far nearly everyone she'd spoken to had quickly offered up the factoid that Genevieve was cheating on her deceased husband.

"Yeah, they were seen having a candlelit dinner together in a pub in Downsmead ages ago. They've never been secretive about it."

"Wasn't Angus upset?"

Edward chuckled. "No, Angus only cared about power and money. He knew Genevieve could never leave him. She doesn't have a penny to her name, he made sure of that. He had power over her, and I think he thought that was more important."

"That sounds terrible."

"He wasn't a very nice man," Edward said.

A tune started playing from within Clara's rucksack. She removed the bag and dug around for her ringing phone. "I'm sorry, that will be Aunt Vee. I'm probably late for dinner."

"No problem," Edward said.

Clara found her phone and quickly answered it. "Sorry I'm late!"

"You can't be late, you didn't give me a time you'd be home," Vanessa replied matter-of-factly. "However, I was considering making dinner soon. If I'm allowed to wait on you?"

"Yes, I'd quite like to be waited on tonight," Clara replied cheekily.

"Oh, good. Well, whenever you're done on that death trap, come home and we'll eat."

"Will do." Clara hung up. She looked at Edward apologetically. "Sorry, time ran away from me. I was going to look at your upcycled furniture, but I need to get back."

"No problem, it's not going anywhere." Edward dug his hands into his pocket. "Like, literally. No one around here buys much."

"It is a bit sleepy. Have you considered a website?"

Edward tilted his head towards the shop behind him. "You try to convince them to enter the technological age. They seem to think they'll get a virus. I don't think their old laptop has enough processing power for a virus."

Clara chuckled. "I'll try and pop by again another day. Maybe I'll convince them."

"Great. By the way, the pub on the corner, the Red Lion, that's where everything happens around here. If you want to socialise or anything, that's the place to go."

Clara followed his gaze and looked at the old, grey stone walls of the local public house. It had been years since she'd stepped foot in such a place. Pubs around her in London were for the old men who didn't feel at home in the trendy bars, cafes, and restaurants where she spent her time. But there weren't many options in a small village like Picklemarsh, which meant if she wanted to chat to anyone socially, she'd have to put on her brave boots and head to the pub.

"Cool, thanks, I'll check it out," she said noncommittally. She was pleased to be issued an invite into the community hub, but she wasn't sure that she was courageous enough to use it just yet.

She adjusted her stance on her bike, preparing her foot on the pedal. "I better get going."

Edward smiled warmly. "Sure, see you around!"

As she cycled away, she couldn't help but think that Edward didn't seem at all like a murderer, no matter what Julian Bridgewater had said. But then, Clara had read enough of her aunt's books to know that the murderer was rarely who you thought it was.

She hoped that Will Ellis would hurry up and crack the case. Knowing that the murderer had been identified and arrested would definitely help to quell the unease she felt bubbling beneath the surface.

Staying in Picklemarsh was meant to relax Clara and help to soothe her anxiety, not make it worse.

12

SETTLING DOWN

Clara put her knife and fork down and let out a tired breath.

"That was delicious, Aunt Vee, thank you so much."

When she'd gotten home, a pasta bake had already been made and was cooking in the oven. It was cheesy, creamy, and probably the most fattening thing she'd eaten in the last year.

Vanessa had prepared salad alongside it. As she chopped the vegetables and placed them in a bowl, she had the look of someone who had never had salad as a side dish before but was making an effort.

Clara appreciated it for her own health and waistline, but also for Vanessa's health. She knew they came from very different times and places when it came to nutrition, but if she could convince her to eat a little healthier, and therefore keep her around a little longer, she'd be a very happy person.

"You're welcome." Vanessa speared another slice of cucumber and looked at it as if it had caused great personal offence. She ate it, regardless.

"I don't think I should encourage you," Clara said, "but I

found out more about the investigation while out on my bike this afternoon."

Vanessa's eyes lit up. "Do tell."

"I saw Sylvester King."

Vanessa looked as irritated as she had at the cucumber. "That fool? What did he have to say for himself?"

"He thinks Felicity Abbot did it. Called her the devil." Clara sipped some water, still not sure if she was upset that Sylvester had accused Felicity, or indeed if she was upset that Felicity may be involved at all. She knew it would be a load lifted from her shoulders if she could just know for certain if the woman she fancied wasn't a murderer.

"Strong words," Vanessa noted. "And what evidence did he provide?"

"None. He said it was obvious. When I asked him what was obvious, he said we'd figure it out eventually."

Vanessa leaned back in her chair, pushing her plate away. She'd eaten all of the pasta bake and four lettuce leaves and two cucumber slices. It was a start that Clara would build on.

"I also saw Edward Milton, and he said that he'd heard from Alf that the police said that the poison was ingested during the dinner. So, it couldn't have been a slow-acting poison that had been given to him the day before, for example. If we believe what Alf says."

Vanessa's eyes widened with interest. "So, the murderer did the deed there and then. As if we needed any more evidence that it was premeditated."

"So, we do trust Alf?" Clara clarified.

"For the meantime," Vanessa agreed. "He is a hub of

information, it's likely that people will share details with him. Hmm, a premeditated murder. Interesting."

"Horrifying," Clara corrected. "And Sylvester King seemed like a bit of a creep."

"He is. Terrible man. Very full of himself, too. Seems to think I'm interested in him; I've been beating him away with a stick ever since I moved in." Vanessa stood up and started to clear the plates away.

"Ah, well, bad news, he said he'd been planning to come over and see you in the next couple of days." Clara stood and helped tidy the dining table.

"Well, let's hope we're out whenever that happens," Vanessa said.

"So, are there any eligible bachelors that you do have your eye on?" Clara asked.

Her aunt snorted a laugh as she filled the dishwasher. "Here?"

"Or anywhere else," Clara said.

Aunt Vee had dated but never settled down. She'd never wanted children and made that clear to anyone who asked if she regretted never having any. Clara knew she preferred being on her own, but she still wanted her aunt to settle down with someone. Even if she was projecting her own desires onto Vanessa.

The idea of settling down filled Clara with glee. To find that special someone, to come home to them every day. It seemed like the best thing one could hope for.

It was not something that Vanessa had ever seemed to yearn for.

"No one worth taking the time over," Vanessa said. "But

I'm old now. I'm stuck in my ways, and I don't want to have to change things for someone. I'm happy as things are."

The last plate was slid into the dishwasher, and Vanessa lifted the door and set the machine. She turned and fixed Clara with a knowing look. "There's only one of us in this house who has a desire to settle down with the *one*, and it's not me."

Clara looked away. She did want to find someone to be with forever. She always threw herself headfirst into relationships and often ended up getting hurt. Dating just wasn't her thing; it was scary and anxiety-inducing. And being gay meant a dramatic reduction in potential partners. She just wanted to get the item ticked off of her to-do list.

Partner: found. Job done.

"I do think you and Felicity Abbot would make a good match," Vanessa pushed.

Her aunt had forever been a matchmaker for her. Clara tentatively came out of the closet when she was fifteen, when she realised that boys were disgusting and girls made her feel something. Vanessa had simply nodded and returned to working on her latest book.

Clara had been worried for days that she'd irreparably damaged their relationship. Not everyone was comfortable with her sexuality, her mother being a prime example of someone who was not only uncomfortable, but also disgusted.

Thankfully, Vanessa had just been in a deep writing phase. When she finally popped back to reality a few days later, she commented that she had discovered a fashionable London gay bar which they would attend as soon as Clara was old enough. And they had. It was a memory that Clara still relished and endured with equal measure nearly a decade later.

Since then, Vanessa had eagerly set Clara up with almost every lesbian or bisexual woman she came across.

"Felicity Abbot may well be a poisoner," Clara pointed out.

"She might not be," Vanessa replied. "She's your kind of woman. Older, has that professional style you seem to like, well-read, educated. The politics might be a bit of an issue, but you're young and you may grow into them."

"Grow into what?" Clara demanded.

"Felicity is…" Vanessa hesitated. "Let's say she's fiscally conservative."

Clara rolled her eyes. That was all she needed, to have a crush on the local Tory. Who may or may not have been a murderer. Was her love life really that barren?

"You think I'll become more fiscally conservative when I'm a real adult?" Clara asked sarcastically.

Vanessa looked at her for a moment and then shook her head. "Probably not. But opposites attract. And you do find her attractive." She turned and walked into the living room.

Clara wanted to deny it, but she couldn't. She knew nothing about Felicity Abbot and had only scarcely seen her, and yet she often thought of her already, as she so frequently did with her crushes.

"We need to go and see Jemima Vos tomorrow," Vanessa called from the other room.

Clara got herself a glass of water and then followed her into the living room. She sat on the sofa opposite her aunt.

"Do we?"

"Yes, she's a missing piece of the puzzle. Someone we've yet to interview," Vanessa said.

"We shouldn't be interviewing anyone," Clara reminded her. "Do you remember that Inspector Ellis was here earlier to tell you just that? Or are you going to conveniently play the old woman card again?"

"There are scant few benefits to being my age," Vanessa said. "I intend to use them as I see fit."

"Including lying to the police?" Clara sipped her water and looked at her aunt over the top of the rim.

"Absolutely." Vanessa picked up a paper from under the coffee table and opened it up. "Let's see. Vos Farm... Vos Farm... here we are. They open at ten o'clock. We'll pop in and get some eggs and such."

"We got eggs today."

"You can never have enough eggs, dear."

"I think you can." Clara put her water on the coaster on the table. "Can you just wander in off the street?"

"Yes, they have a farm shop. They sell all kinds of things, products from the farm, but other things as well. Gifts and knickknacks, that sort of thing."

Clara leaned back and stared out of the window into the garden.

"She likes classical music, you know," Vanessa said.

"Who does?"

"Felicity Abbot."

Clara turned and looked at the newspaper shield. "And how do you know that?"

Vanessa lowered the paper and met her look. "I, my dear, know everything."

13

VOS FARM

After breakfast and some light gardening the next morning, they decided to walk to Vos Farm.

Clara was saddled with carrying the wicker basket and told to hold the fake shopping list that Vanessa had hurriedly created before they set out. It contained items that they'd either purchased the day before or didn't have a need for, but Clara wasn't about to argue. The decision had been made that they were going to the farm shop to speak with Jemima Vos and to get her take on events.

If she were honest, Clara was intrigued by the idea of what they would find out. Angus had been in a legal battle with Anton Vos, but Jemima Vos and Genevieve Chadwick had apparently remained the best of friends. It seemed like an odd situation, but then, so was the common knowledge that Genevieve was having an affair.

"Oh dear," Vanessa said as they turned the corner and walked up the long driveway towards the farm shop.

Clara looked around the sparsely populated car park to

see what had caused the reaction. Her eyes settled on Will Ellis stepping out of his car.

"Good thing you brought all your props," she said, gesturing with her head to the basket and shopping list.

"He better not be here long," Vanessa grumbled.

"He is doing his job," Clara pointed out. "You do want him to solve the case, don't you?"

"If, and that's a big if, he can do it, then yes, of course. But so far, I'm not convinced. Besides, two heads are better than one."

Will had stopped at the end of the driveway. He had his hands in his pockets and was watching them as they approached.

"Good morning," he called out.

"Hello," Clara replied.

Vanessa gave a small nod, clearly irritated that he'd accidentally managed to upset her plans.

"I hope you're not here to speak with Mr and Mrs Vos?" Will asked, looking at her.

"No, we're here for eggs. If we're allowed?" Vanessa queried. "I'd like to make my niece an omelette for dinner. As you can see, she's wasting away."

"Aunt Vee!" Clara admonished. "I keep telling you, I like my weight."

"Skin and bone," Vanessa complained. She looked at Will. "Is an old lady allowed to buy eggs at her local farm shop? Or do I have to get the bus into the nearest town so as to not interfere with your investigation?"

"That won't be necessary, Miss Harrington," Will reassured. "I'm just checking we're all on the same page."

"Quite how you think I have time to investigate this

murder and pen another book, I don't know." Vanessa grabbed the wicker basket from Clara's hand and brushed past Will to enter the courtyard.

Clara looked apologetically at him. "I'm sorry about her."

"It's okay. Has she figured anything else out yet?"

"Oh, she doesn't tell me," she said. "It all ticks away up there, and then it comes out when she wants it to. It's the same whether she's writing, working out a crossword puzzle, or watching a quiz on television."

Will watched Vanessa walking through the courtyard and into the entrance of the farm shop.

"I heard a rumour..." Clara started.

He looked exasperated. "There seem to be a lot of them around here. What did you hear?"

"That Angus Chadwick must have ingested the poison during dinner," she said.

"Who told you that?"

"Does it matter? Everyone will know by now. Finding the source would be pretty difficult."

Will nodded. "Yeah, you're right. Whoever poisoned Angus Chadwick used a fast-acting poison, a type of cyanide. Probably only took thirty minutes to take effect. If you want to feed that back to your aunt..."

"I'll be sure she knows." Clara grinned and walked after Vanessa.

"That doesn't mean she's part of the investigation, though," Will called after her.

"Whatever you say, Inspector."

"Call me Will," he insisted.

Clara chuckled and entered the farm shop. It looked to

be a converted barn with a high, timber-framed roof and plenty of open space. There were a few shelving units, more than she'd seen at the greengrocer's, and there was a decidedly country chic feel to the place.

"Morning," a woman greeted her from behind the counter.

"Hello," Clara replied. She looked around the shop and quickly found Vanessa looking at bottles of wine.

The farm shop had definitely diversified beyond the usual merchandise. There were jams, preserves, fancy biscuits, artisan crisps, bottles of wine, cider, and more. Along the back wall was a delicatessen; upon closer inspection Clara noticed that there seemed to be a butchery operation at Vos Farm. Some of the meat hanging up bore the Vos Farm logo.

Another employee was carving meat. She looked up and nodded to Clara in greeting.

"Take your time browsing," Vanessa said out of the corner of her mouth. "We'll wait for him to leave."

Clara looked behind her aunt to see Will talking to the woman at the counter, who she now assumed was Jemima Vos.

"Okay," she said. "By the way, he confirmed the information about the poison. Definitely ingested during dinner. He said it probably took thirty minutes to kill Angus. He said it was a type of cyanide."

Vanessa pouted.

"What's wrong?" Clara asked.

"It's always cyanide. So unimaginative. I blame Agatha Christie." She turned and started to inspect some artisan bread displayed in various baskets.

Clara shook her head. Some people, it seemed, were never satisfied.

After an age of looking at cakes and pies, Will finally left. He grinned at Clara as he did, obviously aware of Vanessa's intentions.

"He knows what we're up to, you know," Clara told her aunt.

"And yet, he isn't trying to stop us." Vanessa put a baguette in her shopping basket and headed for the counter at the front. "Which means he has no idea and he wants our help."

"I don't think he'd put it quite like that," Clara pointed out.

"Jemima, I was so sorry to hear about the other night," Vanessa greeted the woman at the till. She placed her basket on the desk and started unloading the few absolutely random items she'd gathered in the twenty minutes of bored browsing.

"It's a horrible business," Jemima agreed, her eyes drifting towards Clara.

"This is Clara, my niece," Vanessa introduced them. "This is Jemima Vos, Clara."

"Nice to meet you," Clara said.

Jemima smiled politely at her. "You too. Sorry you are here during all of this. It's usually so quiet and peaceful around here."

"Was that the inspector?" Vanessa asked, indicating the door with a tilt of her head.

"Yes, Inspector Ellis. I think he thinks I have something to do with Angus' death," Jemima explained. "He keeps coming back and asking me more and more questions."

"How very odd. What kind of questions?"

Jemima bit her lip. "I'm really not supposed to say anything."

Vanessa chuckled. "Who would I tell, dear?"

Jemima looked around the shop to check that they were alone and then leaned a little closer. "Well, it's not common knowledge, but there's a large supermarket chain who want to open a store in town. They found a plot of land, and I own it. Angus had been pressuring me for months to agree to sell the land to them. I was considering it, too. He'd agreed to drop all of the charges from the land dispute he is in with Anton. Inspector Ellis was just asking me about that."

"Did you sell the land?" Vanessa asked.

Jemima shook her head. "Anton thought they were offering us far too little for the land, especially considering how desperately they seemed to want it. Julian Bridgewater even offered to buy it off me at one point, no doubt intending to then sell it on to Core Foods—that's the company who own the supermarket chain."

"You didn't accept his offer?" Clara questioned.

Jemima shook her head again. "Anton didn't want to. He hates Angus. Knowing that he wanted the land gave my husband a little power over him. We would have sold it eventually, we'd have to. The court costs from the land dispute have added up, almost bankrupting us. Julian was obviously working with Angus, and we didn't trust him. He's never up to any good."

"Up to no good enough to poison Angus?" Vanessa asked bluntly.

Jemima paused bagging up the goods and thought for a moment. "I don't think so, they've been friends for years. They're as bad as each other. Although Angus is usually the public face of any dodgy dealings they get up to."

"Who do you think did it?" Vanessa asked.

"I've asked myself that time and time again, and I really don't know. Everyone had a motive, and an opportunity. Even me. Not that I'd do that. Poor Pippa and Genevieve, I can't imagine what they're going through." Jemima let out a sigh and then continued to bag the shopping. "It's so strange to think, we all arrived there at seven, and by ten, he was dead."

"It seemed like an odd bunch to all dine together." Vanessa picked up a couple of items from the counter and added them to the diminishing pile of purchases being bagged.

"Oh, it was. Angus said he had an announcement to make. I had no idea who else would be there until I arrived. Felicity Abbot arrived soon after me. I thought that was odd. She's never late, and she seemed distracted."

"What was the announcement?" Clara asked.

"No idea," Jemima said, "he didn't get around to it. We arrived, had some drinks. I helped Genevieve with the meal. We had a starter, and then a main, all premade, of course. We just heated and plated. We broke for cocktails after dinner. Genevieve had been eager to try out some amaretto sours, and we have a new amaretto supplier here, so that worked out rather nicely. People splintered off and were talking in various rooms. We went back into the dining room for dessert, and it was only a couple of minutes after that Angus just collapsed."

"Just like that?" Vanessa asked.

"Yes, straight down and into his dessert. Julian jumped into action and tried to revive him." Jemima put the final item into a bag.

Vanessa placed a newspaper on the counter, adding that to her shopping. "What about everyone else?"

"We were all in shock. Someone called the ambulance—Sylvester, I think. It was pretty quickly clear that Angus was dead. Pippa rushed to her room in tears, Genevieve sat with him, holding his hand, but it was obvious that he was gone. Neither Felicity nor Sylvester seemed that upset, or maybe they were in shock." Jemima raised a shoulder casually. "We all react differently, don't we?"

"We do," Vanessa agreed.

"I'm just pleased that Anton wasn't there. He would have been the number one suspect, and I can't stand the idea of that. Did you know Julian threatened to tell the police that it was Anton?" Jemima said. "I told him not to be so ridiculous. Anyone who knows Anton would know that he could never do such a thing. He never wanted to be in this dispute with Angus. He is a sweet and calm man. Never a raised word. Not like my ex."

"Not a calm man, your ex?" Vanessa asked.

Jemima shook her head. "No, he was a beast of a man. I wasted twelve years of my life on him. I think I only loved him for the first three years. After that, I wanted out, but he blackmailed me to stay. It took me nine years to get the courage to leave him. Can you imagine that, nine years?"

"As you say, we're all different," Vanessa said. "At least you got out when you did. And now you're with Anton."

Jemima smiled. "Yes, I couldn't be without him."

The smile slipped from her face as she seemed to wake up to the fact that she had been talking about something she'd been asked not to. She shook her head.

"Anyway, I shouldn't burden you both with all of this. Just be thankful you weren't there that night."

"Absolutely," Clara said, though she suspected that Vanessa would have liked nothing more than an invite to that particular dinner party. "I hope things get resolved quickly and everything gets back to normal."

"Me too," Jemima agreed. "How long are you staying for?"

Clara hesitated. It hadn't been discussed. She needed a break from the real world, but she didn't know when she'd be ready to go back.

"Quite some time, I hope," Vanessa jumped in. "She's invaluable to me."

"You do just fine without me," Clara told her, gently bumping her shoulder.

"I do, but I want you here," Vanessa told her.

As they set about paying for the shopping and getting ready to leave, Clara had a warm feeling in her heart about the comment.

She'd not given much, if any, thought to what she would do next. Knowing that she had a home with Vanessa for as long as she needed it was a relief. Even if that home was next door to an active murder investigation.

14

ANOTHER PIECE OF THE PUZZLE

They didn't talk much on the walk home, nor as they put the groceries away and made some tea. When they finally sat down in the living room, Vanessa spoke up.

"What do you think about what she said?"

Clara flashed back to years ago, when Vanessa used to help her with her homework. She never gave Clara the answer, preferring to guide her through the process and allow Clara to figure out the truth for herself.

Jemima had said a lot at the farm shop, and Clara was struggling to remember it all. She was jealous of Will and his ever-present notepad. She'd love to jot down some notes as they spoke to people. Instead, she was stuck in a cycle of trying to remember what had been said while still carrying on a normal conversation.

That being said, something did loom in her memory.

"She said that Pippa went to her room in tears, but Genevieve and Edward both say that she's been pretty much unaffected." Clara sipped her tea. "It could have been the shock, I suppose."

"Possibly," Vanessa agreed. "I suspect that we'll need to speak to Pippa to try to find out the truth."

Clara wondered what deception her aunt would come up with next. She wondered if they'd both be dressed as plumbers in terrible fake moustaches.

"She paints," Vanessa explained. "I often see her in the fields painting the view. I'm sure if we go for a stroll around the footpaths, we'll bump into her in no time. She's probably spending more time up there now, out of the way."

"I'm not sure I like the idea of stalking a young woman whose father was recently murdered," Clara admitted.

"Who said anything about stalking? We'll just go for a walk, and if we happen to see her, then we'll say hello. We are neighbours after all."

Clara looked out into the garden. The sun wasn't as bright today, and it looked like the weather might turn. She wished she wasn't so affected by weather, but she could already feel her mood taking a downwards turn.

"Do you really think all of this could be over a plot of land and a supermarket?" she asked.

"Money makes people do all sorts," Vanessa said. "I imagine there is a tidy profit for all involved."

Clara shuddered lightly. She hated the idea that someone would kill someone else, even if they were as terrible as Angus Chadwick seemed. The idea that it was all for money upset her even further.

"She said Felicity was late and seemed distracted," she said.

"She did."

Clara looked at her aunt. "Do you think she did it?"

Vanessa shrugged.

"Seriously, I need to know what you think."

Vanessa put her cup and saucer down on the table to her side and looked like she was giving the question some serious thought. "I can't discount her," she finally said, "but she's not my number one suspect either."

"Who's that?" Clara asked.

There was a tapping on the front door, and Vanessa smiled. "Saved by the bell."

Clara stood up and went to answer the door. As soon as she saw who it was, her heart sank.

"Hello again, my dear," Sylvester King greeted her. He was wearing a three-piece suit and clutched a brass-capped cane in his hand. This one was different to the one she'd seen him with before, indicating that not only did he own a cane, he had a selection of them.

Vanessa must have heard him because Clara didn't have a chance to speak before her aunt was by her side.

"Sylvester, you really must call first. We are having tea," Vanessa told him.

His eyes lit up as he saw her. "Ah, I am sorry! I was just passing and thought I would knock on the chance that you were in and had some time for me." He lowered his cane and leaned on it. "I found out something rather interesting while I was researching my latest book. Something about Angus Chadwick, may he rest in peace."

Clara knew what he was doing, suspected Aunt Vee knew as well, but it was too good a carrot to dangle in front of her.

"Well," Vanessa huffed, "I suppose you might as well come in as you're already here." She stepped back and gestured for him to enter the living room. "I'll get some more tea."

"I'll get it!" Clara quickly interjected. There was no way she wanted to be left alone with Sylvester King while her aunt made tea. No, she'd much rather be hiding in the kitchen for as long as socially acceptable.

"Coward," Vanessa whispered to her.

Clara wasn't going to deny it. She breezed into the kitchen and set up a tray the way Aunt Vee would. Tea wasn't a hastily made and consumed beverage for the older woman; it was more of a ritual. It had to be served correctly, no corners cut.

Clara had to admit that she'd missed the calming effect of the ritual. She'd gotten used to making mugs of tea and mindlessly guzzling them, or worse, putting it into a take-away mug to drink on the train into the office.

It was nice to take her time and get everything ready on the tea tray. She could hear the distant sound of Sylvester and Vanessa talking, but nothing in detail. There was something about Sylvester King that rubbed her the wrong way.

Yes, he was inappropriate with his staring, but he was hardly the only man, or woman, to do that. There was something beneath the surface that Clara didn't like. The fact that he could be a murderer on top of that made him all the more avoidable in her eyes.

When she couldn't delay it any longer, she sighed and picked up the tray and took it into the living room. Sylvester had sat himself next to Vanessa on one of the sofas, a blessing, as it meant that Clara wouldn't have to sit beside him.

She placed the tea tray down, and Vanessa leaned forward to serve them.

"And so, I ferreted a little deeper into it," Sylvester continued, not even acknowledging Clara's return.

"I presume you discovered something very interesting, as you're dragging this out so much?" Vanessa asked.

Sylvester brushed off the criticism. "It was all in the archives in the council office, buried under many other documents. Misfiled, of course."

"Biscuit?" Vanessa offered the plate of fruit shortcakes, clearly not wanting Sylvester to feel as if she were at all interested in the story that he was dragging out for all its worth.

"No, thank you. Angus Chadwick's father, Albert, was a pacifist, which is all well and good, but not when the country… was at war," Sylvester finished with a flourish. He took the teacup and looked meaningfully at Vanessa.

"So, he was a conscientious objector?" she asked.

"Yes." Sylvester nodded quickly. "Such shame for a proud family like the Chadwicks. Buried away in the council office. But I found it. I always do."

"And Angus knew that you'd found this information about his father, I presume?" Vanessa asked, pouring Clara a fresh cup of tea and handing it to her.

"Yes. I'd written the story, but the publisher wanted to see if there were any pictures of Albert. Well, I had to speak to Angus about it, and I wanted to see if I could get a quote from him."

"I assume he wasn't pleased?" Vanessa added extra sugar to her tea, a clear sign that she was fed up with the man.

"Livid," Sylvester declared, almost pleased with himself. "Tried to blackmail me."

"Oh yes?" Vanessa asked.

"Yes. Of course, that boy from the police found out

about that, and now he thinks that I'm the killer. As if we don't all know the perpetrator already."

"How did he try to blackmail you?" Vanessa asked, backtracking the conversation a little.

Sylvester rolled his eyes. "Such childish behaviour. He told me he was planning to add a new sewage tank for one of the cottages attached to one of the farms. That tank would need to be sunk right by my garden, not a hundred metres away. You can imagine the stench of a hot summer's evening. But I wouldn't be moved. The public deserve to know."

"Do they?" Clara asked.

Sylvester looked at her, seemingly for the first time since she entered the room. He seemed confused; whether it was the question itself or the fact that she'd chosen to speak up at all, she didn't know.

"Of course, it's the history of the village," he said.

"Hardly relevant today," Clara argued. "If Angus' father didn't want to go to war, then surely that is family business? And is it so terrible that someone doesn't want to go to war and kill people?"

"If everyone held that attitude, we'd all be speaking German," Sylvester told her.

"You have a theory as to who killed Angus?" Vanessa asked, effectively stopping the argument in its tracks.

"Yes, it's obvious," Sylvester said. He sat back and looked a little miffed that someone had dared to stand up to him. Clara didn't care. She was also a pacifist and didn't think for one second that anyone should be publicly shamed for being one. If more people were pacifists, there wouldn't be any wars to win.

"Do enlighten us," Vanessa instructed.

"Felicity Abbot," he said. "Very obvious."

"How did you come to that conclusion?" Vanessa asked. "Where's the smoking gun?"

"She hated Angus, wanted his job; they'd been at odds for weeks about some planning permission thing. She was late to dinner, seemed very flustered, probably had no idea we'd all be there—"

"Why were you there?" Vanessa interrupted.

"I'm sorry?"

"It seems like an odd bunch," she said. "A neighbour, family members, accountant, co-worker, you. Why were you all there?"

Sylvester laughed. "We were all summoned by the high and mighty council chairman. He said he had an announcement to make. I wasn't going to attend, but I'll admit that curiosity got the better of me in the end."

"What was the announcement?" Clara asked. She'd heard so much about the announcement. Though it was clear from the others that Angus never got time to say what he'd gathered them all for, someone must have had a clue what the announcement would be about.

"He keeled over before he had time to say," Sylvester replied.

"You didn't have an idea what it was about?" Clara pressed.

"None. It was very sudden." Sylvester sipped his tea. "I bet he is looking down now and regretting he invited Felicity."

"What evidence do you have that it was her? Actual evidence?" Clara asked.

Sylvester looked uncomfortable. "You do *know*, don't you?"

Clara tilted her head. "Know what?"

"She's... one of them."

Clara could feel the anger building, but she had to be sure it was warranted before she erupted. "One of who?"

"Gay," Sylvester explained, a nod punctuating the one word like a gunshot.

"And?" Clara demanded.

Vanessa held up her hand before Clara could really get started. "Sylvester, I don't appreciate that backwards kind of nonsensical speak in my home."

He laughed. Actually laughed. "Come on, Vanessa, you know she is."

"I do know she is. I meant that I won't allow homophobic comments in my home. How dare you come in here and say such things? So Felicity Abbot is gay; so what? That doesn't make her a murderer. The very thought that you think it does is, frankly, disgraceful and an embarrassment for you. She's an excellent local councillor and a decent member of the community. Her sexuality has nothing to do with anyone but her. How dare you."

Tears were threatening to spill from Clara's eyes. Despite the staunch defence of her aunt, she still felt sickened by the attack, even though it wasn't directed at her. She'd come across homophobia before, but it blindsided her each and every time. How could be people so cruel? How could they judge based upon nothing but sexual preference?

She put her teacup down. "I'm sorry, but I have something I need to do."

Vanessa looked up at her apologetically. "Okay, call me when you can."

Clara nodded, relieved that her aunt wasn't going to out her in front of the vile man or request that she stay in his presence a moment longer. She walked around the table and pressed a kiss to her cheek.

"I won't be out long," she promised.

She left the room without saying a word to Sylvester King. She had no desire to speak to nor see the man ever again.

15

A CRASH AND SOME TEA

Clara sped away on her bike. She had no idea of direction, she just wanted to get away from Sylvester King and his cruel words. Even though the sentiment wasn't directed at her, she'd felt the blow personally.

Homophobia wasn't anything new, but Clara just couldn't understand why people insisted on hating one another. It was as if society did all it could to categorise people, and then hate on anyone who was different.

Of course, Clara wasn't entirely immune to it herself. She often judged others, but she was aware of the flaw and took steps to correct her behaviour when she found herself doing it. She had no right to judge someone who was overweight, or a parent who seemingly couldn't control their child.

She referred to it as staying in her own lane—not looking around to see what she could evaluate in others, but rather focusing on herself and what she was doing. It was a learning curve. She wasn't perfect, but at least she was trying.

Her anger meant she wasn't paying attention to the road

in front of her, so when she saw a white car reversing out of a driveway and into the road, she didn't have much time to react. She swung the handlebars to the side to avoid a direct collision, and hopefully avoid being run over.

There was no way she could apply her brakes in time. Instead she ended up being suddenly stopped by a large hedge on the side of the road. She fell from the bike and tumbled to the ground, cursing herself for not wearing her bike helmet as she hit the tarmac.

She squeezed her eyes shut, wondering what would come next. Would the car hit her regardless? Would her bike land on her? Her senses were in overdrive, and she struggled to focus on a single one.

"Are you okay?" she heard a female voice ask. She was too shaken up to answer; the truth was she didn't yet know.

"Clara?"

She looked up and blinked at the figure standing over her. Concern was etched onto Felicity Abbot's face. Clara knew she needed to get herself together and reply soon.

"I'm okay." She tried to stand up but winced at a sharp pain in her knee.

Felicity took hold of her arm. "Careful. You took a big tumble there, give yourself a moment."

Clara nodded softly in agreement and looked around. Charity seemed to be in one piece, and Felicity's car seemed to be unscathed.

"I'm sorry," Clara whispered, suddenly feeling embarrassed.

If she'd been paying more attention, this would never have happened. It was obviously her fault; she'd been flying down the narrow country lane without a thought for anyone else, too wrapped up in her own anger to even think about safe road usage.

"I wasn't paying attention."

"Never mind that, are you okay?" Felicity asked, her grip on Clara's arm was firm.

"I think so."

Felicity took a gentle hold of her chin and tilted her face away. "You have a scratch; I'd like to clean that up for you. And make sure you're okay. That was quite the fall."

"I don't do anything by halves," Clara said.

Felicity chuckled. "I'll put the car back on the drive, and then we'll get your bike and put it in the garden. Then I'll make some tea and we'll look at that cut."

"You don't need to do that. I'm sure you're busy."

"Not particularly," Felicity replied. She loosened her grip on Clara's arm. "Can you stand?"

Clara took a couple of tentative steps and was relieved that the pain in her knee was already dissipating. "Yes, I feel much better."

Felicity didn't look convinced but still let go of Clara's arm. Clara watched as Felicity went back to her car and drove it forward into the driveway. She picked up her bike and was surprised at how well it had dealt with being hurled into an unforgiving hedge.

Better than she'd managed. She wheeled it over to the house, realising that Felicity wasn't the kind of person who would let her go on her merry way without being sure that she was all right.

That thought warmed Clara; it also terrified her. Her crushes on older, unobtainable women were always better from afar. When she got closer to them, she rambled, made ridiculous statements, or sat and stared at them. Sometimes all three.

Her palms were sweating, and not from the bike crash.

"Let me survive this," she muttered to herself as she propped the bike up against the wall.

"Sorry?" Felicity appeared behind her, a frown on her face.

"Nothing! Just… just talking to myself," Clara said. "It's a thing I do."

Felicity looked at her for a moment before she turned and headed towards the house. Clara wanted to kick herself. Instead she slowly followed Felicity.

It wasn't a turn-of-the-century cottage like so many of the other properties she'd seen in Picklemarsh. It was a newer building, still in keeping with the surroundings, but larger and more modern.

The garden wasn't an overgrown country style like she had seen elsewhere. It was a strip of well-maintained lawn and a couple of flower beds which mainly contained rose-bushes. A pear tree framed the side of the garden. It was the space of someone who didn't spend too much time gardening, but still wanted to fit in with their surroundings. It was a practical garden, and it suited Felicity to a tee.

Clara stepped into the house and closed the front door behind her. She took a calming breath and promised herself that she would keep her ridiculous crush under control. It always happened like this, a sudden bolt from the blue, her mind focused with laser precision on someone she could never be with. It was as if her heart were playing games with her.

"Tea?" Felicity offered.

Clara walked into the kitchen, a bright and modern space decorated in whites and light woods. "I don't want to be a bother."

"Tea?" Felicity asked again, more insistent this time.

Clara smiled. "Yes, please. Thank you."

Felicity smiled in return. She gestured to the kitchen table. "Take a seat, I'll get the first aid kit."

Clara frowned. "It's not that bad, is it?"

Felicity gestured to a mirror that hung on the wall. Clara peered at her reflection and was shocked to see she had a nasty-looking gash on her cheek. And her hair was a mess. She quickly finger-combed it so she didn't look like such a disaster.

Clara looked around the kitchen while Felicity was absent. It didn't look like the kitchen of a murderer, but then, she didn't really know what she was looking for. She refused to believe that Felicity had anything to do with Angus' death, but she knew she had no valid reason for that. Only hope.

"Sit down," Felicity instructed as she returned with a small, green plastic box.

Clara took a seat, not quite knowing why she instantly did what this almost-stranger told her to do. Felicity had an authority about her that Clara could only dream of having.

"You don't seem like the sort to not pay attention when on your bike," Felicity said. "Or the sort to not wear a cycle helmet." She opened the first aid kit and pulled out a sealed wipe.

"I was upset," Clara confessed. "I'm sorry."

"Don't be." Felicity opened the packet and unfolded the

wipe. "We all have moments like that. I'm just glad you managed to react when you did. I'm fond of my car."

Clara choked out a small laugh.

"But you really must wear a helmet in the future. You were lucky today," Felicity told her.

"I know, I… it was silly."

"Well, everything ended up fine in the end," Felicity said. "And, as a personal favour, I'd like it very much if you didn't tell everyone that I nearly ran you over."

"You didn't nearly run me over," Clara corrected. "I nearly rode into you."

"It will soon be distorted. Before you know it, I'll be cast as Cruella de Vil, racing down narrow streets with a maniacal look in my eye as I attempt to run you off the road."

Clara frowned. "Then I'll correct them."

Felicity took Clara's chin and angled her face so that she could see more clearly. She gently cleansed the dirty cut with the antiseptic wipe. "It wouldn't matter."

"Why not?"

"Because I'm not everyone's favourite person." Felicity tilted her head to examine her handiwork. "Being on the council means saying no to many people. After a few years, you end up with a lot of people disliking you. And… there are other reasons."

"What other reasons?" Clara asked, her voice barely above a whisper as they were sitting so close.

"I'm different." Felicity sorted through the various sticking plasters, deciding which size was best.

"I'm different, too," Clara said.

Felicity hummed, not grasping her meaning. She picked out a plaster and unwrapped it. She softly positioned it and then ran a firm finger around the edge to ensure it was fixed in place.

"As good as new," she said. "Now for that tea."

"I don't want to be a bother," Clara said.

"No bother." Felicity got two plain white mugs from a cupboard and placed them by the kettle. "Sugar? Milk?"

"No sugar, a little milk, please."

Felicity set to making the drinks. "Are you enjoying Picklemarsh? Murder aside, of course?"

Clara cringed at the casual way Felicity spoke of the murder of her boss and colleague.

"It's okay. I could have done without the murder," Clara replied.

"You and me both," Felicity said.

"Some people say you did it," Clara admitted.

"I know." Felicity put the two mugs on the table. "I'm not upset that Angus is dead, I'm not mourning his loss, and therefore I must have been the one who killed him. Disliking someone and being pleased to be rid of them are quite different to actually taking their life."

"Can't you pretend to be sad that he's dead?" Clara asked.

Felicity considered that for a moment. "I suppose I could, but that would be a lie. He wasn't a nice man. I mean, I hope he didn't suffer, and from what I saw, he didn't. It seemed relatively quick and painless. Ordinarily, I'd feel sorry for his family, but they disliked him, too."

Clara couldn't fault the logic, but there was something a little cold about Felicity's approach. Clara wondered if she was on the spectrum; it would explain a lot. It would mean that she hadn't meant to be unfeeling, she was just extremely practical.

"Who do you think did it?" Clara asked.

"Not a clue," Felicity said. She took a sip of tea. "Many people would like to see Angus out of the way, but I can't imagine who would have the courage, or the stupidity, to actually murder him."

"Why were you there that night?"

"Is this an interview in your official capacity as part of the police investigation?" Felicity asked with a wry grin.

Clara laughed. "I'm nothing to do with the police investigation," she confessed.

"I know. Bold of your aunt to say that you were."

"Yes, she's like that."

"Who does *she* think did it?" Felicity queried.

"I don't know. She's still mulling it over."

"I think I read a couple of her books, many years ago," Felicity said. "Crime isn't really my thing, but when she moved into the village there was a bit of chatter about her. I remembered one about a kidnap plot? A little girl at the seaside, I believe?"

Clara nodded. "She won an award for that one."

"It was very good," Felicity agreed. She leaned forward and straightened Clara's jacket lapel, which was still in disarray from her fall. "Oh…"

Clara watched as Felicity's gaze fell upon the rainbow pin that she kept on her lapel. Clara couldn't see what she was doing, but it felt like she was running her thumb over the indentations of the pin.

"I used to have one of these," Felicity said. "I'm not sure where it is now."

Clara swallowed hard. "Y-you should find it. And wear it."

Felicity ruffled her nose. "Not around here. Not at my age."

Clara wanted to argue the point, but she was almost hyperventilating at the close quarters they'd just shared. A little voice told her to get out; she didn't know Felicity, and here she was sharing tea with her. It wasn't helping her crush, and there was still the very real possibility that she had killed Angus Chadwick.

"I have to go," Clara blurted out.

"Oh, I'm sorry. I shouldn't have kept you," Felicity said, standing up as Clara did. "Are you sure you're okay?"

"Yes, I'm… I'm fine." Clara nodded firmly. "Thank you for patching me up. And the tea. I appreciate it."

She was already nearly out of the kitchen, desperate for escape. Her anxiety was growing in leaps and bounds and she knew she needed to get away from Felicity before she embarrassed herself further.

"You're most welcome. Remember a helmet next time," Felicity said.

"I will. And I'll be more careful, I promise." Clara opened the front door and clapped her eyes on Charity, her salvation and her escape.

"See that you are," Felicity said.

Clara hurried over to the bike and wheeled it through the garden. She tossed a hurried goodbye over her shoulder, looked both ways, and cycled away as quickly as she could.

16

AN INSPECTOR CALLS

Clara hoped that Sylvester was gone when she returned to Chadwick Lodge. She really had no desire to see the man. Ever again, if she could help it. If he was still there, then she'd go to her room and wait. It was rude, but she'd had an emotionally trying day and was not interested in making things worse.

She parked Charity up by the garden wall and took a calming breath as she approached the front door. Before she had time to slip her key into the lock, it opened.

"He's gone, don't worry," Vanessa told her. "Come on in."

Clara pocketed her key and entered the cottage. "I'm sorry."

"Don't apologise. He was in the wrong, not you. I'm sorry for what he said. I honestly didn't know he held those views. I put him right after you left; he won't be making the mistake of uttering such nonsense ever again."

Clara closed the door behind her. "Thank you, I appreciate that. I thought I was used to it, but I guess I'm not."

"You should never become used to that kind of talk." Vanessa frowned. "What happened to your cheek?"

Clara had almost forgotten the sticking plaster on her face. "Let's sit down," she suggested.

They took their customary seats in the living room, and Clara sucked in a lungful of air as she thought about what to say and where to even start. She was in for an earbashing because of her carelessness on her bike.

"I took a little spill," she admitted. "Off my bike."

Vanessa's eyebrows rose, but she remained silent, waiting to hear everything before she passed judgement.

"I wasn't paying attention. I was going down a lane, and a car reversed out of a driveway. I turned to avoid it and ended up in a bush instead. I'm absolutely fine, though."

"Who nearly mowed you down?"

"No one nearly mowed me down, but they did help me up and make sure I was okay."

Vanessa looked at her pointedly, awaiting an answer to her question.

"Felicity Abbot," Clara said softly.

"Felicity nearly ran you over?" Vanessa asked in surprise.

"No, I almost hit Felicity's car because I wasn't paying attention. And then she helped me up."

Vanessa's expression morphed into a sideways smile. "I see."

"It's not amusing," Clara told her.

"I know. I just... I know you find her attractive, but throwing yourself off your bike isn't the usual way one meets people, dear."

"Aunt Vee!" Clara complained. "That's not what happened."

"Were you hurt?" Vanessa asked.

"Just a minor scratch," Clara said, gesturing to her cheek.

"Hmm. Lucky. And why were you not wearing your helmet?" Vanessa asked, her expression extremely serious.

"I forgot it in my hurry to leave," Clara admitted. "It won't happen again."

"See that it doesn't." There was no mistaking the tone. Concern and a hint of anger. Clara didn't blame her one bit.

"It won't. I'm okay."

"You're clearly not okay." Vanessa gestured to the cut on her cheek.

"Felicity cleaned it and put a plaster on it."

"Did she now?" Vanessa was smiling again. "Oh, to be a fly on that wall…"

"I don't know why I tell you things," Clara grumbled.

"I'm sorry, I'm sorry." Vanessa held up her hands apologetically. "It's just rather amusing."

"For you, maybe." Clara rested her chin in the palm of her hand. "I'm mortified. First, I was the clumsy idiot who fell off her bike. Then I could hardly get a word out. Then I ran away."

Vanessa's expression softened. "Ran away?"

"I just… I got embarrassed, and it all got too much for me. I said I had to go and ran. My anxiety was spiking, you know?"

Vanessa nodded. Despite never having personally suffered from anxiety issues, she did understand the condition and was considerate of it. Clara had often felt weak when her anxiety hit and prevented her from doing things, sometimes the simplest of things, but her aunt had always been supportive.

"Did she say anything valuable about the investigation?" Vanessa asked, smoothly swerving the conversation onto a somewhat safer topic.

"She said she didn't do it, but she's aware that people are saying she did."

"What did she say about that?"

"She didn't seem to care. She doesn't care that he is dead, and she doesn't want to pretend that she does. She said he wasn't a nice man. She also said she wouldn't have wanted him to suffer, but it looked quick and painless. Oh, and she said she'd ordinarily feel sorry for the family, but they didn't like him either."

"Well, that's true."

Clara huffed. "I just feel so bad. I mean, no one seems to care that this man was murdered."

"People care that he was murdered. They just don't mind that he is gone," Vanessa corrected her. "Which tells you a lot about the man. And presumably about the person who killed him."

"Felicity said she didn't know who killed him. She said lots of people had a motive, but she didn't know who would be brave enough or stupid enough to do it."

"Do you believe her?"

Clara opened, and then closed her mouth. She didn't know. She *wanted* to believe Felicity, but that was a very different thing.

There was a loud rap on the door.

"My, my." Vanessa stood up. "We are popular lately."

Clara watched her go. She reached her hand up to touch the plaster, remembering soft, warm fingers on her cheek. Pushing Felicity out of her mind now was going to be impossible.

"Look who has come to see us, Clara." Vanessa walked back into the living room, Will Ellis trailed behind her. "Presumably going to tell me off for shopping."

Vanessa dropped into the armchair and gestured for Will to take a seat.

Will sat on the edge of the sofa. He turned to Clara to nod in greeting, then frowned. "Been in the wars?"

"Just a scratch," Clara explained. She pointed to Vanessa. "Is she in trouble?"

Will chuckled. "Actually, no. I came to ask for your assistance, if you're still willing to give it?"

Vanessa looked as surprised as Clara felt.

"Well, we are rather busy, Inspector," Vanessa lied.

"No, we're not. What do you need?" Clara asked. She wasn't about to let Vanessa cause Will to rescind the offer with some misspoken words.

Will smiled at her, obviously grateful for the middleman. "Resources are thin on the ground, and I don't mind admitting that this case isn't an easy one. It's got us running in circles, and the longer I spend here, the less time I have for other cases. If I can get this resolved quickly, it's better for everyone. I'm sure you'd both agree."

"Absolutely," Clara said.

"The crime scene at the manor has been closed off to the family since the murder, while we gathered evidence and such. Tomorrow morning, we'll be allowing them back into the room. Before that happens, I wondered if you'd be able to cast your expert eye over the scene?" Will turned to Vanessa. "If you have time."

Clara could see the glint of smug satisfaction in Aunt Vee's eye.

"I believe we could make some time," Vanessa said. "Now, for example, would be good for us."

Will had barely finished his nod of agreement before Vanessa had jumped to her feet. She left the room with a promise to return shortly.

"Thank you," Clara said. "For asking her."

"It would be foolish not to," he confessed. "She knows all the suspects and has a lot more knowledge of the local area, personalities, and issues. And she's one of the best crime writers in Britain."

"She'd say the world," Clara pointed out. "I take it you're no closer to coming up with a prime suspect if you're asking us to get involved?"

Will shook his head. "We have no forensic evidence to look at, only the body. He was poisoned during the course of dinner. The poison was ingested, but we don't know how or when. At this point, I'll take all the help I can get. With every day, the trail grows colder, and people have more time to dispose of any evidence. I don't want this investigation to stall."

Clara could understand that. She couldn't imagine the kind of pressure Will was under. The family, the local community, his bosses, everyone wanted this mystery solved.

"I did ask the Met about your aunt's advisory work with Chief Inspector Ludlow," Will said. "Interestingly, they'd never heard of him."

"How strange," Clara said. She stood up. "I think I'll just go and get a warmer sweater. Excuse me."

"She's a piece of work, your aunt," Will called after her.

"No idea what you're talking about," Clara claimed.

17

CHADWICK MANOR

Clara stood in the doorway to the dining room at Chadwick Manor. It was a grand room with oak-panelled walls and oil paintings of ancestors looking down at the large table which occupied the majority of the room.

It looked eerily abandoned. The chairs were in disarray, left exactly how they had been that evening. The table had been cleared of the plates and cutlery, but coasters and centrepieces remained, and the candles were burnt halfway down.

Clara thought it reminiscent of a haunted house.

"We took all of the food, drink, plates, bowls, cutlery, et cetera away to be analysed," Will explained. "No trace of poison in anything."

Vanessa had circled the table three times, taking in everything from every angle possible. Clara had no idea what she was looking for, or if she'd found it.

Will approached the table. "Here, at the head of the table, was Angus Chadwick. On his right was his wife, Genevieve. To his left, Julian Bridgewater. Next to Julian was Felicity Abbot; next to her, Sylvester King. Next to Genevieve was Pippa; beside her was Jemima Vos." Will walked around the table, indicating each chair as he went. He leaned on the back of the chair at the opposite end to where Angus had sat.

"He collapsed just before ten o'clock. An ambulance was summoned at ten; Mr King made the call. Attempts were made to revive the deceased by Julian Bridgewater, but those attempts had stopped by the time the ambulance arrived at twenty past."

"So, it was either visibly obvious that he wouldn't be revived," Vanessa said, "or Julian knew that it was fruitless for other reasons."

She walked over to the long, antique sideboard which filled most of the wall at the end of the room. On top of the sideboard was all of the cutlery, crockery, and glassware which had been analysed by the police.

"We have a number of timelines of events for the evening," Will said, "from all of the suspects. Unfortunately, after the main course was consumed, the diners all had cocktails and seemed to scatter. Everyone spoke with Angus at some point in the forty minutes before he was killed, some privately in his office, some in the sitting room."

"Six wine glasses," Vanessa said.

"Sorry?" Will walked over to the sideboard.

"There were seven diners, and yet there are six wine glasses," Vanessa said.

Clara joined them and looked at the wine glasses, counting them for herself.

"A water glass," Vanessa continued, tapping the edge of a

tumbler, "would indicate that someone wasn't drinking with dinner."

"That's true," Will agreed.

"However, that doesn't explain why there are only five cocktail glasses," Vanessa continued. "If you're drinking wine with dinner, then surely you'd also indulge in a cocktail?"

"Weren't all of these people driving?" Clara asked.

"We're in the country now, dear, people are stupid," Vanessa stated. She turned to Will. "You say the party dispersed into the sitting room and the office?"

Will nodded and gestured for Vanessa to follow him.

Clara walked around the dining room table, wondering what the atmosphere had been like on the night of the murder. Had tempers been frayed? Had people been polite? What was Angus' announcement? There were no answers to be found.

She left the room and followed the sound of quiet chatter into what appeared to be Angus' office. It was a typical, old-style office, exactly what she expected the man of the manor to have. A large desk with a green leather top sat in front of a large window; behind it was a large, leather office chair. Papers were strewn everywhere over the desk in what some might call organised chaos, but what Clara thought of as a mess.

There was an uncomfortable-looking sofa and two leather tub chairs. The room was again surrounded by oil paintings of long-deceased relatives. Clara was glad that tradition was no longer a popular one. She'd hate to eat her breakfast, or conduct her work, with the beady eyes of her grandparents staring down at her.

"After dinner, separately and privately, Angus spoke with

Felicity, Julian, and Sylvester privately in this room," Will explained. "Each time, the door was closed."

Vanessa pointed at the paperwork on the desk. "I assume someone has been through all of this?"

"Yes, and believe me, we put it back the way we found it. There was nothing that pointed towards a motive—general council documents, various legal documents to do with businesses he owned or had invested in. Paperwork, basically, lots and lots of paperwork."

"He needs a secretary," Clara commented.

"He had one," Vanessa said. "In fact, he's had several. They all leave within a few weeks, from what I've heard."

Will took out his notepad and jotted that down.

Vanessa turned and regarded the window, running her hand over the four sides before looking up at the curtain pole. She then turned and started to inspect the filing cabinet and knickknacks that sat on top of it.

"Could someone have broken in, poisoned him, and then left again?" Clara asked.

"Unlikely," Will said. "All of the windows are locked from the inside, and there are perimeter alarms on all the doors and windows. He wasn't alone at any point in the evening, except to go to the bathroom once. No one else saw anyone hanging around."

"Well, that answers that," Vanessa said.

Clara turned to see her aunt leaning into the open fire-place and pointing at something. She looked more closely at the burnt-down wood and soot. Something glinted in the blackness.

"Is that… glass?" Clara asked.

"It is." Vanessa stood up. "If I'm not mistaken, that's the missing cocktail glass."

Will gently manoeuvred Clara to one side and knelt down. He pulled a thick, plastic evidence bag from his inner jacket pocket and then some gloves. He snapped on the gloves and set about extracting the glass pieces from the fireplace. Slowly, piece by piece, he pulled out the remains of an ornate-looking glass, similar to the saucer-style glasses that were on the sideboard in the dining room.

It did indeed look like the missing glass. Vanessa was looking exceptionally pleased with herself.

"Good spot," Will said. He placed the glass pieces in the evidence bag carefully. "I'll kill whoever searched this room, right after I call someone to come and bike this to the lab immediately."

18

PIPPA CHADWICK

Clara and Vanessa left Will to it and entered the sitting room to see what they could find in there.

"I'm getting a picture of what happened that night," Vanessa said, "though, there's one big question that doesn't make any sense."

"Really?" Clara said. "What's that?"

"All in good time. I don't want to let the question know it's beaten me. Best not to voice it."

Clara wasn't about to argue with Vanessa's methods. If she honestly felt that an abstract idea such as a question had awareness, that was fine. As long as she solved the murder mystery, the perpetrator was arrested, and things went back to whatever normal was.

The sitting room contained yet more uncomfortable-looking sofas. Clara had often thought that grand, old stately homes never looked like particularly pleasant places to live, and Chadwick Manor was no different. Everything was extremely formal, almost stuffy. There were no modern-day comforts of home.

No television. No soft cushions or deep pile rugs.

The rest of the house was probably different, but the downstairs areas were solely for presenting to guests. That sent a shiver through Clara's spine. To live in a place so sterile and devoid of life would be horrible.

"Hmm." Vanessa crouched down by one of the sofas, pulling her niece's attention away from her dismal thoughts.

"What have you found?" Clara asked.

Beside the sofa was a round table with a shelf full of magazines. Vanessa pointed to one in the middle of the stack.

"What about it?"

"It's not sitting correctly; it's been open at a certain page for a long time. Probably bent around and left like it for a while." Vanessa eased the magazine out of the middle of the pile.

It was a high society women's magazine, all about hosting the perfect party, centrepieces for tables, and cocktail dresses that cost more than Clara would ever dream of spending on a one-night-only item of clothing.

Vanessa gently opened the magazine, encouraging it to open where it desired. The page it fell open to was focused on being the perfect hostess, complete with articles about dinner services from Royal Doulton, printed invitations, cocktail recipes, and gift bags.

"Interesting," Vanessa murmured.

"What is?" Clara leaned over her shoulder to look for herself.

"Many things." Vanessa closed the magazine and looked at the front. "Even more interesting."

"What?" Clara insisted.

"This magazine is two years old—"

"Miss Harrington?"

They both looked up. A young girl in her early to mid-twenties stood in the doorway. She wore a pair of tailored black trousers and a white blouse. Her hair was stylish, though clumsy, and she looked tired.

"Hello, Pippa," Vanessa greeted her. "Sorry if we disturbed you, the Inspector wanted my help. This is my niece, Clara."

Pippa looked at Clara and offered a little wave.

"I'm sorry for your loss," Clara said. She'd lost her father and couldn't imagine it being anything other than devastating. But the more she learnt about Angus Chadwick, the more she realised that wouldn't be the case for everyone.

"Thank you." Pippa walked into the room. "Is Inspector Ellis so useless that he's just asking anyone off the street to help with the investigation?"

"I have some experience in these matters," Vanessa said.

Pippa looked apologetic. "I'm sorry, that was rude. I'm just very tired and emotional at the moment. Things have been... strange."

"I can only imagine," Vanessa said.

"I don't miss him, though," Pippa explained. "I hated him for years, everyone knew it, there's no point in saying otherwise now."

Pippa sat on a sofa and rested her arm over the back of it. A picture of young, wilful defiance. Clara remembered the look from her own youth, claiming all sorts of nonsense that she wished were true. She realised how mature she had become and how immature Pippa still was.

"I did hear that you were at odds." Vanessa sat on the sofa opposite Pippa.

"He told me, and anyone who would listen, that Edward wasn't good enough for me," Pippa explained. "He tried to ban us from seeing each other, but I wouldn't allow that. Just because he doesn't know what love is."

"You don't think your father loved you?" Vanessa asked.

Pippa shook her head. "I don't think he knew how to love people at all. He trapped my mother in a loveless marriage. He might have thought he was doing the right thing by me, but he made me miserable."

"It must have been hard living here with him," Clara said.

Pippa nodded. "I know what you're thinking—why didn't I move? Leave home? It's harder than you might think. Edward's family is here, and my father runs the village. Ran, he ran the village."

"Why does that make it hard?" Clara asked.

"He would have been furious if I left. He wanted me to stay here, to be a Chadwick and marry into money. Be the lady of the manor." She gestured around the room. "Literally. He used his influence on people to make sure no one offered me a job. There's not a single person in Picklemarsh who would hire me because they were scared of what my father would do to them."

Clara couldn't believe that a man would impede his daughter's progress in life in such a way, all to keep her at home and under his control.

"Being a Chadwick is the worst thing that ever happened to me," Pippa said. "Everyone in town hates me or is frightened of me. I'm glad he's gone. Hopefully, I can get my life back now. Hopefully, I'll convince Edward to leave here one day."

"May I ask you about the night Angus died?" Vanessa asked.

Pippa nodded. "Sure. I don't think I can help, but ask away."

"Why are there only six wine glasses on the sideboard? Was someone not drinking wine that night?"

"Yes, me," Pippa explained. "I don't drink. I grew up seeing what it did to my father, so I never started. I had water all night."

"Everyone else drank alcohol? Wine and later cocktails?" Vanessa confirmed.

"Yes. You have to drink to live in Picklemarsh. You'll go mad otherwise."

Vanessa chuckled. "That's true. Was there anything strange about that night?"

Pippa sat forward, her elbows on her knees and her head resting on her hands. "Everything was strange about that night."

"How so?" Clara asked.

"It was unlike my father to gather so many people he didn't really like. I didn't want to attend, but he insisted, said he had an announcement and I needed to be there. I assumed it was something to do with work, but, if so, then I don't know why Jemima came. It was all a bit odd."

"What was the announcement?" Clara asked, assuming she already knew the answer.

Pippa shrugged. "He never got to say."

"Was there anything else that happened?"

Pippa stood up and walked over to the window. "It was

like any other time he had business colleagues over to the house, loud arguing. At one point he went into his office with Felicity. They were shouting. I heard him say he'd stop her, stop her doing what I don't know. But that was quite common; they fought a lot about council stuff. They were always fighting."

"Do you have any ideas what it might have been about?" Clara asked, hoping something specific might stick out in Pippa's memory.

Pippa shook her head. "No idea, as I say, it happened a lot. And he argued with Sylvester King as well. More shouting. There was always shouting. You see why it's so hard when the police ask if he had any enemies."

She wrapped her arms around herself and turned to look at Vanessa. "I'm sorry, I'm not much help."

Vanessa waved the apology away. "Nonsense, you're a great deal of help. I'm just sorry that this has happened. I hope you haven't been cooped up in here since it happened? You need to make sure you get some fresh air, some distraction."

"I'm trying," Pippa admitted. "I go up to the hiking path off Cherrywood Farm trail every morning to paint. That helps."

Clara knew that nugget of information would be filed away, enabling Vanessa to 'just be passing through' at a later date.

Will entered the room. "I have a bike coming to get the new evidence," he announced. His eyes settled on Pippa, and he nodded. "Miss Chadwick."

"Inspector," she said disdainfully. "Excuse me, I have a headache and wish to go to my room." She brushed past

Will and left the sitting room as quickly as she could without running.

Will looked a little embarrassed. "We're often not well liked by the family after an event like this," he explained.

"I think poor Pippa Chadwick has had a bit of a lifetime of not liking or trusting people," Vanessa said. "Probably why she is so keen on Edward. He's a nice lad."

"He has yet to be excluded from my enquiries," Will pointed out.

"I don't believe you've managed to exclude anyone from your enquiries yet. Am I right, Inspector Ellis?" Vanessa replied with a small smirk.

"I don't think you've solved it yet either, Miss Harrington." Will grinned back.

"Not yet, but I am very nearly there."

Clara looked at her aunt and couldn't detect a lie. She wondered what she had seen that Clara and Will had missed.

"Tell me, Inspector, everyone says they were gathered here because Angus Chadwick had an announcement to make. Do you know what that announcement was?" Vanessa asked, preventing Will from quizzing her on her theories.

"No," he admitted. "He died before he could make the announcement. We questioned everyone and searched his office, but we couldn't tell what the announcement was going to be. His wife was told it was something to do with a new supermarket being built, but we have no evidence of that. And it seemed like a strange group to assemble for such an announcement. Looks like we'll never know."

Vanessa stood up. "Well, thank you for showing us the

crime scene. I'm going to sleep on it, and I'll let you know what I come up with."

Before Will could say another word, she left the sitting room. Will turned and looked at Clara. "Does she have anything?"

"I think so," Clara said. "It's hard to be sure."

"And she'll let us know?" he asked.

She smiled. "Oh, trust me, she'll let you know. With great pleasure."

He bit his lip and looked out into the hallway. "Okay, good. I have a bad feeling about this one. Something is not quite right, and I just can't put my finger on it."

Clara had to admit she felt the same. It was a scene directly from one of her aunt's books—a dinner party in a large country estate, a host of suspects, each with a motive and the opportunity.

"Hopefully the glass will be your breakthrough," she said. "Of course, if it is. you'll never hear the end of it."

"I'll take that punishment," Will admitted. His gaze lowered to her collar, and she saw his eyes widen slightly at the rainbow lapel pin she still wore. She wondered what would come next, how their relationship would change.

"Where did you get that pin?" he asked.

"My aunt got it for me," Clara said.

"I think I might get one for my little brother, he just came out. I'll look online."

"That's a nice gesture." Clara smiled. Coming out was never dull; she really never knew what kind of reaction she was going to get. Thankfully, there were more people like Will in the world than there were Sylvester Kings.

"Clara!" Vanessa called out from the front of the house.

She sounded impatient, presumably eager to get home and gossip.

"Sorry, I better go," Clara said. "Obviously, she'll let you know if she comes up with anything."

"Thank you, both of you," Will said.

Clara jogged a little along the hallway towards the front door. Aunt Vee stood on the driveway, jerking her head towards the lodge.

"Come on."

"I'm coming," Clara told her. She jogged to catch up. "You're so impatient."

"The real question is, is Pippa trying to throw us off the case?" Vanessa asked as they walked side by side down the path towards the cottage.

"How so?"

"It's a poisoning case, and there's the matter of the missing glass. If you were going to poison someone, then wouldn't you make all efforts to ensure you didn't accidentally ingest it? Including not drinking that evening."

"She makes it sound like she never drinks," Clara pointed out.

"Quite," Vanessa agreed. "And that is information we need to verify."

"Edward would know," Clara said.

"That he would. Although, there's a possibility he is in on it. And, if he is, then of course he would lie for his girlfriend."

Clara opened her mouth to reply but closed it again when she saw movement up ahead. "Is that someone at the lodge?"

Vanessa looked up. "Yes, it is."

They walked a little closer, just as the visitor was apparently giving up and walking away from the cottage and back to their car.

"Well, look who it is," Vanessa said, pure glee clear in her tone. "That's someone who could tell us if Pippa is really teetotal or not."

"Don't you dare! She's leaving, let her go," Clara begged.

"Felicity!" Vanessa called out, waving her arm to attract the woman's attention. Felicity turned around and spotted them. She smiled and waved in return.

"Phew, we nearly missed her," Vanessa said. "Good thing you saw her."

"I hate you," Clara mumbled, attempting to look like she didn't want to throttle her matchmaker aunt as they approached the end of Chadwick Manor's drive.

19

A LITTLE HISTORY

Clara couldn't believe that she'd dropped her wallet in the hedge and hadn't even noticed. Any embarrassment she felt before paled into insignificance now that Felicity had driven over to return it.

"I expect you've been looking for this," Felicity had commented once they'd gotten closer.

The truth was that Clara hadn't even realised she'd taken it with her, and therefore had no idea it was missing. But she nodded her agreement and thanked Felicity profusely before apologising for wasting yet more of her valuable time.

The whole mortifying episode could have ended there if Vanessa hadn't invited, nay, demanded, Felicity come into the house and have some tea and some cake.

Admittedly, they were overloaded with cake after the pointless shopping trip to Vos Farm. Still, just as Clara had breathed a sigh of relief that Felicity was leaving her to curl up and die from embarrassment, Vanessa struck.

Now Clara stood in the kitchen with her aunt, trying to help her prepare a tray of tea and cakes for the three of them. It was definitely a job for one, but Clara was quite happy to hang out in the kitchen and provide practically zero help, rather than go and sit in the living room where Felicity was.

"Go in there," Vanessa whispered.

"No!" Clara argued.

"Don't make me get your baby photos out."

Clara gasped. "You wouldn't."

"Go and talk to her and you won't need to find out."

Clara stared at Aunt Vee for a moment before she huffed and stormed away. She took a deep breath before she entered the living room, trying to calm herself and make sure she appeared to be a normal human being rather than the bag of nerves and anxiety she actually was.

"Thank you so much for returning my wallet," she said as she entered the room.

Felicity sat on the sofa, in the place Clara had come to consider her own. She'd only been there a few days, but already that sofa had been designated hers, the other seemed to belong to Aunt Vee.

Clara sat on the same sofa, at the other end. She immediately regretted it as it meant she could smell Felicity's perfume and also had to turn ninety degrees to look at her.

"Not at all. I saw something on the ground and realised you'd be looking for it." Felicity turned and looked out of the window and into the back garden. "Did I see you coming from the manor?"

"Yes, Will wanted Aunt Vee's opinion on something," Clara said.

"Ah, then I'm to assume the murder at Chadwick Manor

will soon not only be solved but also available in all good bookstores?"

"I'm rather fond of the title *Death Before Dessert*," Vanessa said as she came into the room with a loaded tea tray.

Clara jumped up and helped her. Once the tray was safely on the coffee table, Vanessa shooed her away and started to serve them all.

"But I'm afraid we're no closer to solving it, unless you remember something that will crack the case?" She looked to Felicity.

Felicity shook her head. "Sorry, nothing more than what I've already told you and the inspector." She took the proffered cup and saucer and thanked Vanessa.

"Ah, well," Vanessa said. She poured a cup for Clara and placed it down in front of her. "It's only a distraction really, something to train one's brain and distract Clara from thinking about her recent break-up. Well, I say recent, it was a while ago now, wasn't it?"

Clara nearly dropped the cup. This was classic Aunt Vee meddling; Clara should have been prepared for it, but she wasn't.

"Um... yeah..." She could feel her cheeks heating up.

"Jenny," Vanessa said the name with disgust. "Terrible woman."

"Aunt Vee," Clara said with a warning tone, although she had to admit she agreed. She paused, wondering when that had happened. She'd been missing Jenny right up until a few days ago. Suddenly she realised, in all the murderous hullaballoo, she hadn't thought of her as often.

"Clara is the very best girlfriend," Vanessa said. "Caring, thoughtful, intelligent, cultured—"

"Aunt Vee," Clara repeated, hoping to stop her as quickly as possible.

"But that sometimes means people who aren't worthy of her end up hurting her," Vanessa continued. "I keep telling her that you have to go through a few people like that before you find the one. Don't I, dear?"

Clara sadly nodded, consigned to her fate of sitting and listening to Vanessa's words.

"I agree," Felicity said, surprising Clara.

"I thought you would," Vanessa said. "You're very sensible. I'm sure you feel the same, that as you get older you find out what kind of people you need to look for. Don't let Clara's young age fool you; she's very mature and very wise."

Clara willed a hole to swallow her up. Or an earthquake. Or even the doorbell to ring. Even a visit from Sylvester King would be better than this.

"I noticed," Felicity agreed. "And you're right, you have to date a few people who are wrong for you to find out who is right for you."

"Precisely. This Jenny, not good enough for my Clara," Vanessa stated. "Yes, she looked right on paper, older, settled, attractive, but I don't think she knew how to love. I say that with respect, but I think for whatever reason, she struggled with that."

"That's a shame, everyone deserves love, above all else," Felicity said. She turned to Clara. "I'm sorry your relationship ended, but I'm sure someone better is right around the corner."

Clara felt her mouth slip open a tiny amount as Felicity

looked at her with those big, beautiful eyes. She'd happily noticed that Felicity reacted ever so slightly when Vanessa had described Jenny as older and settled.

"Th-thank you," Clara stuttered.

"Obviously, I'm useless to her," Vanessa said. "Do you know where she might go to meet women around here? I suppose there aren't many places."

Felicity shook her head. "Nowhere local, you'd have to go into town. I'm not really sure, I'm a bit too old for that scene."

Clara focused on sipping her tea, hoping that her bright red cheeks could be attributed to the hot drink. She cast a sideways glance at Felicity as she delicately picked at the slice of cake Vanessa had given her. She didn't seem at all uncomfortable with the discussion.

"Nonsense," Vanessa said, still in matchmaking mode. "I think Jenny is about your age. You met her at a bar, didn't you, Clara?"

Clara had actually met Jenny through a friend, but she knew exactly what her aunt was up to. It was a casual way to show that Clara had dated someone Felicity's age. Sneaky, but casual.

"Yes," she said, hating the lie but knowing that it was a fairly trivial one.

"Maybe you two can go into town together one day in the future. Isn't that what girls do these days? Anyway, I mustn't go on. Clara will kill me once you've left. And we're trying to forget about Jenny, not talk more about her. Tell me, are you aware that Pippa Chadwick doesn't drink?"

Felicity blinked at the change of conversation but

nodded. "That's right. She's never drunk at all as far as I know."

"Well, good for her," Vanessa said. "So many young people getting drunk every weekend. It's nice to hear that some young people are able to stay away. Clara drinks in moderation, don't you, dear?"

"I've considered starting day-drinking since moving in here," Clara quipped.

Felicity chuckled. "You two seem very close."

"She's my favourite niece," Vanessa said.

"I'm her *only* niece," Clara corrected. "But yes, she's very important to me. Even when she is embarrassing me."

"Her mother is useless," Vanessa explained. "Had her far too young and quickly realised she wasn't cut out to be a mother, or a wife."

Clara lowered her gaze to her lap. She hated to speak ill of her mother, but it was all true. She wanted to love the woman and have a normal relationship with her, but she knew that was never going to happen. Even so, it was still something that Clara just couldn't accept.

Vanessa didn't have a good word to say about her mother, and Clara couldn't blame her.

"She fought endlessly with my brother," Vanessa was saying, "and finally, finally, they agreed it would be better for everyone if they divorced. Clara was eleven. I asked if she wanted to stay with me for a while to give her some stability while she was at a critical point in her studies."

"That was very kind of you," Felicity said.

"I adored her. She's turned into a beast as an adult," Vanessa joked. "If you could have seen her then. Well, I do have some photos…"

"Aunt Vee," Clara warned.

"Another time." Vanessa winked at Felicity. "It was supposed to be temporary, but she ended up staying with me for four years. She had an opportunity to board at school after that, but she was close by, so we saw each other frequently."

"It sounds like things worked out for the best," Felicity said.

"They did," Clara agreed. She shared a smiled with her aunt. She'd never be able to explain just how grateful she was for being taken in during that time in her life.

Vanessa deftly turned the subject to some local council business, and they casually spoke about the local community for the next half an hour until Felicity said she had to leave. It had been strangely nice, mortifying at times, but as Clara relaxed, she'd found she had actually enjoyed spending time getting to know Felicity a little better.

Not that she was going to let Vanessa know that.

"There'll be a second murder in this village if you do that again," Clara complained the instant they'd finished waving Felicity off. She ushered Aunt Vee into the cottage and closed the door.

"I don't know what you mean," Vanessa said. "I'm being, what do they call it? Your wingman?"

"I don't want you to be my wingman, I don't want to talk about my ex with Felicity, and I don't want to go to a gay club in town with her," Clara informed her.

"Well, of course you don't. But now she knows you're a lesbian, you're single, you like older women, and you're in the market for someone new. And you know that she's also single, believes in love, and is very interested in you."

"That is entirely not the point, you shouldn't ha— What did you say?"

"She knows you're a lesbian, single, that you lik—"

"Not that. You said she's very interested in me?" Clara chased after her aunt, who had entered the garden and picked up a watering can.

"Yes, she couldn't stop looking at you. I know those eyes," Vanessa claimed. "You two would have taken years to get to this point without my tiny little interference."

"She was looking at me?" Clara asked.

Vanessa grinned at her but didn't say a word. When she turned on the tap and started to fill the watering can, Clara knew she'd not get any more out of her on the matter.

20

A CLOSE ENCOUNTER

Clara bit into the crisp, wholemeal toast with a tiny scraping of low-fat spread and sighed in pleasure. She'd gone to bed early, slept well, and was having a lazy morning. Well, as lazy as it got for the Harringtons.

She'd ignored Vanessa's clattering around that morning, put her headphones in, and listened to an audiobook until eight-thirty. Then she came downstairs in her pyjamas and was now enjoying a breakfast of green tea and toast.

Vanessa was writing in the living room, and all was quiet and peaceful. Clara picked up the local newspaper from the kitchen table and leafed through it. Most of it was taken up with the murder of Angus Chadwick, but towards the back she found some other articles.

She still hadn't decided how long she'd stay in Pickle-marsh. Some friends from London had texted her and asked to meet up, but she knew they meant meet in London and she just wasn't ready for that yet. She loved London, but like a bad break-up, she needed some time away.

The phone rang, and Clara heard Vanessa answer the call.

She knew there was no hurry for her to decide what to do with her life next, or even when to do it, but she felt unsettled, as if everything were impermanent. It was a feeling she wasn't fond of.

Vanessa entered the kitchen and pointed at Clara's outfit. "You might want to get dressed."

"Is someone coming over?"

"Yes, Inspector Ellis is coming over to take us to Julian Bridgewater's house." She placed a cup and saucer in the dishwasher. "He's dead."

She said it in a casual way, the way someone would comment that it was raining outside. So much so that Clara felt for sure that she'd misheard. "I'm sorry, what?"

"Julian Bridgewater's dead," Vanessa clarified. "Murdered. His housekeeper found him this morning. Inspector Ellis would like my opinion, presumably because I found that glass yesterday. He knows an eagle eye when he sees one."

Clara was reeling. "Julian Bridgewater has been murdered?"

"Apparently so. Come on, you need to get dressed. You can't go to a murder scene with a teddy bear holding a balloon emblazoned on your chest."

Vanessa left the room, presumably going to get herself ready.

"Come to visit," Clara muttered. "It will be nice. We'll go for walks in the countryside. It will be like a holiday."

She stood up and put her plate and cup in the dishwasher, eating the rest of her toast in two quick bites.

Clara gasped and turned around, her hand instinctively covering her mouth. She wasn't sure what she'd expected to see, but a dead body collapsed over a desk with a very prominent knife sticking out of its back wasn't it.

"Sorry, I should have warned you," Will apologised.

"It's… fine," she muttered. "I just… wow, yeah."

Vanessa didn't seem to have any concerns about being so close to a murdered body. She entered the room at speed and made a beeline for the corpse.

"Found this morning?" Vanessa asked.

"Yes, but first look tells us he was murdered late last night," Will replied.

"It's rather bold," Vanessa commented. "Not as subtle as poisoning. Either our one murderer became frustrated or frightened. Or… we have two murderers."

Clara spun around. "Two? In such a small village?"

"Stranger things have happened," Vanessa assured her.

"Maybe I will go back to London," Clara muttered. She glanced at poor Julian Bridgewater again and promptly turned away.

"The window was left open," Will explained. He approached the large sash window behind the desk. "We suspect the killer escaped this way. Possibly they entered this way as well."

Vanessa looked at the window and then the body. She nodded. "The killer could easily look through the window, see their target, and creep up on him. There was clearly no struggle. Whoever did this perhaps wasn't sure if they'd be able to overpower him in a confrontation," she said thoughtfully.

Clara turned away and started to look around the office. Much like Angus Chadwick's, it was a masculine space, with dark furnishings and dim lighting. There was a row of filing cabinets along one wall. Clara tried a handle, and the drawer slid open. She ran her hands over the tabs displaying name after name of individuals and corporations. Julian Bridgewater seemed to know everyone in Picklemarsh.

Her fingers grazed the name of Felicity Abbot. Part of her was eager to look inside the file, but a bigger part of her knew that desire had nothing to do with the case.

"He seemed to work with everyone," Will said as he approached Clara. "Narrowing down a list of suspects might not be easy if we don't find some evidence."

"Do you think it's connected to Angus' murder?" Clara asked.

"I hope so," he replied. "I wouldn't like to think that they weren't connected and that everyone in Picklemarsh has decided it's okay to commit murder. I can tell you now that the first person I will be speaking with is Edward Milton."

"Why?"

"During the last conversation I had with Mr Bridgewater, he told me that he suspected Edward Milton of killing Angus Chadwick."

"He told me the same thing. It doesn't mean anything," Clara defended the man.

"Maybe not, but I still have to investigate."

She closed the filing cabinet draw and turned away. Edward seemed so nice. She hated the idea that he was a suspect, but she logically knew that the investigation had to follow the clues. And being nice wasn't an indication of innocence, as much as she may have liked that to be the case. Felicity, nice as Clara considered her to be, was as likely to be suspected as mean old Sylvester King, no matter how much she hated that fact.

Will's phone rang. "I'll be in the hall," he said as he took the call.

Clara looked at Vanessa, who was trying to peer around Julian's body to look at the desk.

"This was an act of passion," Vanessa said sombrely. "Someone wanted Julian dead and acted, quickly and without thinking."

"Presumably that means they'll be fairly easy to catch," Clara said.

"Not necessarily. Many of these cases rely on knowing who had a motive, finding a key piece of evidence, witnesses." Vanessa stood up and pointed to the knife. "That looks very clean to me. I wouldn't be surprised if the killer thought to wear gloves. Who wouldn't these days, no matter how angry you were? Maybe there is some DNA somewhere, but I've not seen any hairs, a drop of blood, nothing. Witnesses? Well. We're in the middle of nowhere. At night."

Will came back into the room. "That was the station. They ran a check, there was an outgoing call from the desk landline at ten forty-three last night. It seems Mr Bridgewater called Miss Abbot. I'll need to go and speak with her."

"Well, we're done here anyway. I'll call you if I think of anything," Vanessa said. She gave Julian's body one last look and then left the room, Clara hurried after her, saying a speedy farewell to Will as she did.

"Do you want a lift back home?" Will called out.

"We'll walk," Vanessa said. "Time to think."

A few minutes later they were walking along the quiet road. Vanessa's face held a deep frown; Clara knew this second murder had thrown a spanner into her original thoughts.

"Does that complicate matters?" she asked.

"It does indeed. Now we need to decide how these two murders are connected. I can't imagine that they're not. But do we treat them as two pieces in the same puzzle, or two different puzzles all together?"

Clara wasn't entirely sure what Vanessa meant. She'd never been particularly good at logical or lateral puzzles. The closest she got to these kinds of questions was when watching a murder mystery on the television. Even then, she was most often wrong in her assumptions.

She decided to allow her aunt time to think, unravelling her headphones from around her phone and putting the earbuds into her ears. She selected some nice, calming music and tried to enjoy the walk back home, pushing all thoughts of Picklemarsh and its murders out of her mind.

21

CLOSING-DOWN SALE

They were walking through the high street when Vanessa tugged at Clara's sleeve. Clara paused the music and removed an earbud.

"What is it?" she asked.

Vanessa gestured towards the other side of the road. Milton Furnishings shop' window was covered in hastily created 'closing down' signs.

"Let's go inside," Vanessa suggested, already crossing the road.

Clara followed her aunt as she walked straight into the shop and looked around for someone to speak to.

"Hello?" Vanessa called out.

A man appeared from a backroom and smiled. "Hello Vanessa, how are you?"

"Tom, I'm well. I just saw your signs. Are you really closing down?"

Tom Milton was undoubtedly Edward's father; he had the same kind smile.

"I'm afraid so. It's been in the cards for a while now. The

rents have been going up and up. We had a visit from Bridgewater Accountants yesterday. A creditor made a demand that we just can't pay. We'll be declaring bankruptcy by the end of the week," Tom explained.

"I'm so sorry to hear that," Vanessa said. "Was it Julian who came here?"

Tom laughed lightly. "No, he wouldn't waste his time coming to see us. No, he sent some underling to do his dirty work. I do blame him for this, though."

"You do?" Vanessa queried. "How so?"

"He's dealt with our finances since we first set up," Tom explained. "Convincing us to take out all kind of insurances, so we've been paying into these schemes for years. Now that we need them, none of them adequately cover us. What is the point in having income protection insurance if it doesn't pay out when you need it to?"

Vanessa shook her head. "Scandalous, some of these insurance companies. You have to really read the fine print to see what they do and what they don't cover. But who understands what all that legal jargon means?"

"Precisely. We trusted Julian, but it seems he just made us pay into a number of completely useless insurance schemes. Lining someone's pocket but not mine." Tom ran a hand through his hair. "Sorry, I shouldn't be complaining. People have it far worse. It's just been a very hard couple of days. Edward is taking it the worst; we hadn't really told him we'd been having problems, so it's come as a bit of a shock to him."

"Oh, the poor lad," Vanessa said.

"Yes, we're going to have to move away from the area. No point in staying here if we don't have the shop. We'll need new jobs, and commuting from here just isn't feasible. He was furious when we explained everything to him."

"I can imagine. I bet he didn't have a good word to say about Julian either?" Vanessa asked.

"No. But there's been bad blood there for years. Did you know that Edward worked for Julian for a year after school?"

"No, I wasn't aware. Did it not go well?" Vanessa asked, idly looking at a dining chair as she did.

"Terrible. Julian thought he was lazy, Edward thought Julian was a task master. He stuck it out for a year, then he left and got the job at the train station. Said he'd rather stand out in all weather and wait for the five trains a day than spend another minute working with Julian." Tom shook his head.

The shop door opened, and Felicity stepped in. She wore yet another power suit and was clutching a handful of papers to her chest. Her eyes widened slightly as she saw everyone deep in conversation. "I'm sorry to intrude." She smiled at Clara, and Clara returned the gesture.

"Not at all, we were just passing," Vanessa said.

"I'm just dropping off some paperwork. We'll be so sorry to see you go, Tom," Felicity said. She walked over to him and handed over the bundles of paper.

"I just hope you get someone in here again quickly," Tom said. "You see some high streets left with empty shopfronts. It's the beginning of the end, when that happens."

Vanessa took Clara's shoulders and pointed her towards the door. "We best be leaving. Sorry again, Tom. Send Janet my best wishes."

"I will, and thank you for all your custom!" Tom said.

Everyone exchanged farewells, and Clara and Vanessa quickly left.

"He doesn't know about Julian," Clara said.

"No," Vanessa agreed. "I think we should go and speak to Edward Milton before the grapevine finds its way to him."

"Julian and Edward have history; do you think that's why Julian pointed the finger at him?" Clara asked as they hurried towards the train station.

"Possibly, or maybe it's the reason that Edward killed him," Vanessa replied.

22

SEARCHING FOR LOST PROPERTY

"What lie will you tell this time?" Clara asked her aunt, only half joking. So far, she had been pulled into nearly every lie Vanessa had told in her attempts to gather information from potential suspects.

She guessed the visit to the train station to speak with Edward Milton would be no different.

"You'll find out when I tell it," Vanessa told her.

Clara let out a soft sigh.

They entered the old Victorian station house, no more than a lobby with one door out to the street and one to the platforms. Off each side of the lobby was a door; one led to the ticket office, which had long since been abandoned in favour of the automatic ticket machines. The other simply had a 'private' sign on it. Presumably storage or office space, Clara thought.

"Why don't you tell me now? So I don't look so shocked," she suggested.

"Because then you'd try to talk me out of it and tell me that lying is wrong."

Clara couldn't fault Aunt Vee's logic. That was exactly what she'd do. Still, she'd like to know what ridiculous lie was about to be thrust upon her.

They entered the platform, which was completely empty save for Edward, who was sweeping a few stray leaves into a dustpan. He saw them enter and stood up straight.

"The ten-thirteen has been cancelled," he said apologetically.

"We're not here for a train," Vanessa said. "When Clara arrived the other day, she might have dropped a ring. Have you seen one?"

Edward shook his head. "No, nothing here."

"She was positive she had it on the journey, but I was quite sure I didn't see it when she arrived. It might have fallen on the platform somewhere, or in Big Dave's taxi."

Edward looked around. "Well, I didn't see anything, but you're welcome to look around. And we can check the lost property box, in case someone handed it in when I was off."

"Wonderful. Clara, would you like to look around? You know where you alighted the train." Vanessa turned to Edward. "Did you hear the news?"

Edward raised an eyebrow. "I don't think so?"

"Julian Bridgewater is dead," Vanessa said without preamble.

Clara abandoned her half-hearted search for her non-existent ring and waited for Edward's reaction. Not a lot changed in his features. He didn't seem surprised; he certainly didn't seem upset.

"Oh, well, I can't say I'm sad to hear that," he said.

"He was murdered," Vanessa explained.

This time Edward did look shocked. "Murdered? Another poisoning?"

"No, a far more direct method," Vanessa said, without elaborating too much.

Clara wondered if Edward had killed Julian and was pretending to not know anything about it, distracting them by asking if it was poisoning when he knew the truth all too well. Great. She'd become paranoid.

"Not surprised," Edward said, shrugging his shoulder and returning to sweeping errant leaves. "He'd been involved in dodgy dealings for years. He's as bad as Angus was."

"What kind of dodgy dealings?" Clara asked.

"He controls everyone's finances," Edward explained. "Very badly, I might add. He's sold off property and land for his own benefit. He's just bankrupted my parents because he wants the shop on the high street for a friend."

"How do you know that?" Vanessa asked.

"You hear a lot when you work at the station. I've seen people arriving from other towns to look at the high street. They say they knew a shop would become available soon." Edward shook his head. "He's a monster. Was. Was a monster."

Vanessa looked at him for a couple of silent moments before she nodded. "Right, well, I need to check that lost property box. I assume it's in the ticket office?"

"Yeah, it's open, just go straight in," Edward said.

"Thank you. Clara, you stay here and see if you can see anything on the platform."

There was a subtle insistence to Vanessa's tone that only a close relative would detect. Clara heard it loud and clear and realised that Vanessa was going to do more than just look in the lost property box.

"Edward can help you. You know how terrible you are at looking for things," Vanessa added.

"Okay, Aunt Vee," Clara mumbled, wondering why all of these lies needed to embarrass her in some way.

Vanessa left them to it, and Clara began her imaginary search for her ring. Edward followed behind her.

"Do you know where you might have lost it?" he asked.

"Not a clue," Clara admitted.

"Maybe it rolled under these benches?" Edward crouched and started to look.

Clara bent down and pretended to do the same. "I'm sorry about your parents' shop," she said.

"So am I. It's a shame Julian's dead. I would have liked to kill him myself."

"Don't say that." Clara shook her head sadly. "No matter how terrible a person is, you shouldn't joke about killing them."

Edward sighed. "Yeah, I know. I'm just… so angry."

"Well, now's a dangerous time to say such things. You might end up being a suspect," Clara pointed out.

Edward chuckled. "I'm probably already a suspect. Male, twenties, knew the victim, definitely have a motive. Who else are they going to suspect? Old Mrs Keane?"

He stood up and sat down heavily on the bench.

"Everyone turned on me overnight. I went from being the nice young man from the railway, to the probable murderer of Angus Chadwick. Now, I'll be accused of being a double murderer."

"Then tell people you are innocent," Clara implored. "Do you have an alibi?"

"When was Julian killed?"

"Last night, I think."

Edward laughed bitterly. "Yeah, I was at home. Alone. Might as well hand myself in to hurry along the process."

Clara sat on the bench next to him. She wanted to tell him everything would be okay or give him some advice, but she had no idea what to suggest. He was right. From a logical profiling point of view, he was one of the prime suspects.

She'd hate to be in Edward Milton's shoes right now.

"I'm sorry," she said. "I wish I could help."

"It's okay. It's not your fault. I'm just sorry that all of this is happening when you're supposed to be visiting your aunt. It's not a great time for it."

Clara noticed that Edward's knee was bouncing up and down and that he'd glanced at his watch several times. She didn't know what it meant. Perhaps he was waiting for an arriving train? Perhaps he was nervous? She wasn't as good at this as her aunt.

"She likes a good mystery," Clara said.

"Does she have a theory?" he asked.

She rolled her shoulder. "Not sure, she doesn't say."

"Clara! I found it! Come on, let's go," Vanessa called from the station house building.

"Well, that's good news," Edward said, standing up. "About the ring, I mean."

Clara stood. "Yeah, I'm… glad she's found it. I better go. Take care."

"You, too." Edward picked up the dustpan and brush and continued his work.

Clara looked at him one last time before turning and walking along the platform. Vanessa may have enjoyed a good mystery, but Clara struggled with it. She didn't know who to trust, and that drove her mad.

She wanted to either trust people or not. Knowing that she had probably spoken to a liar and a murderer over the last couple of days was hard to swallow. Realising that she had no idea who that was was far, far worse.

23

THE FLIMSIEST OF APOLOGIES

"So, you found my ring?" Clara asked sarcastically once they were outside the train station.

Vanessa sighed. "You'll make a terrible investigator if you're not willing to tell a little white lie every now and then."

"I never said I wanted to be an investigator," Clara reminded her. "What were you up to? I'm guessing that you weren't really looking in the lost property box."

"I did have a brief look in there, out of curiosity, but my main aim was to investigate Edward's personal belongings."

Clara shook her head. "That's a breach of his rights, you know."

"And if I were to say I found blood on his jacket sleeve?" Vanessa asked.

Clara stopped dead in shock. "You did?"

Vanessa shrugged. "No, but I might have done. And then you'd have been very glad that I had checked. But I found nothing. Nothing that would prove his innocence or his guilt."

They started walking again.

"However, he did confirm his personal hatred for Julian," Vanessa pointed out. "Which is, of course, a motive."

"Sounds like a lot of people didn't like Julian," Clara said. "Is there anyone else who is intensely disliked locally who we might want to warn? We should call them up, tell them that there's been a spate of murders, mainly of really terrible people, so they better get out of town."

"Well, there is one that springs to mind." Vanessa's voice lowered, and Clara followed her gaze. Across the road was Sylvester King, and he was walking straight towards them.

"Oh god," Clara muttered.

"I'll get rid of him quickly," Vanessa promised.

Sylvester raised his arm to attract their attention. Not that he needed to. His salmon-pink suit, complete with tie, tie pin, and a white hat, meant he stood out without any additional movement required.

"My dear, I'm so glad I bumped into you," Sylvester said as he approached, addressing Clara.

They stopped walking, and Sylvester stood in front of them, leaning heavily on his cane, this one adorned with a brass eagle. Clara felt residual anger building within her. She didn't want to be anywhere near him.

"Spit it out, Sylvester, we're in a hurry," Vanessa said.

"Of course, of course, I just wanted to say how terribly sorry I am. You see, I'm an old man. I grew up in a very different world."

As apologies went, it was terrible. Clara had heard it before, as if somehow the fact that someone was beyond a certain year, or grew up in a certain time, made it perfectly natural for them to hate someone they'd never met just based upon a part of that person they didn't like. Sexuality, skin colour, whatever they'd decided was 'wrong'.

"You're sorry?" Clara asked.

"Yes, very much so." Sylvester started to smile, apparently believing that his over the top apology was going to work.

"For what?" Clara asked. She folded her arms.

"For what I said," he clarified, looking at her as if she were simple.

"And what did you say?" she asked.

"Well, you know what I said. Let's not go over old ground, let's just try to move on. I'm apologising in good faith, and—"

"But I'm not sure what you're apologising for. Are you apologising because I took offence, or because you are aware that you said something offensive?" Clara asked. "Because the way you were talking before sounded to me like you have deep-seated homophobia running through your blood. But now you are apologising, and I have to wonder where this sudden one-eighty came from?"

He opened and closed his mouth a couple of times before turning to face Vanessa. "Dear, help me explain what I mean."

Vanessa held her hands up. "Don't entangle me in this."

"But you understand that I—"

"To be honest, Sylvester," Vanessa continued, "I think that an apology is earned over time. And perhaps now isn't the time as tempers are running a little hot?"

"Well, if Clara were willing to simply accept my apology—"

"Why should she?" Vanessa interrupted. "You came into my house with your backwards, hateful views, and now you feel an apology and an explanation that you're *old* is enough. Well, I'm old, too, Sylvester. I don't go around hating people because of who they love. Or where they are from. Or the colour of their skin. You can't say whatever you like and then write it off later just because you're old. The fact that you think you can will surely not help you to have your apology accepted. So, may I suggest that we leave this discussion until another day?"

Clara watched Sylvester practically wilt under Vanessa's intense stare. He looked at a loss for what to say next, and Clara couldn't help but enjoy the fact that he'd had the wind taken out of his sails, even if only for a brief while.

"In other news," Vanessa said, "have you heard about Julian Bridgewater?"

Sylvester's large eyebrows collided in a frown.

"Murdered," she said. "Last night."

Sylvester's eyes widened. "Murdered?"

"Yes. I'm sure the police will be in touch to ask you what you were doing last night."

"Me? Why me?" he asked.

"Because it's probably connected to Angus Chadwick's death, and you're a suspect in that murder, are you not?"

"I was at home last night," Sylvester said.

"I'm sure that's what everyone will be saying," Vanessa said. "Anyway, we really must be going."

She gently took hold of Clara's arm, and they both stepped around Sylvester and continued their journey up the lane towards the high street.

"Do you think it was him?" Clara asked.

"I wouldn't have thought so," Vanessa admitted. "I don't think he is the sort to murder someone with a knife. I'd say he probably isn't strong enough. And the cane isn't for show. He does struggle with his hip, so I can't see him climbing in through Julian's office window without being seen or heard."

"He's going to keep apologising to me until I accept his apology, isn't he?" Clara asked.

"Probably. But that doesn't mean you have to accept it. Especially if you don't think he means it."

"Do you think he means it?"

Vanessa mulled over the question for a few seconds. "I think I don't really understand people with that kind of prejudice. I don't know if it's something that can be untaught."

Clara tended to agree.

"Maybe we should take a more scenic walk back?" Vanessa suggested. "Avoid the Sylvesters of this world and possibly even bump into Pippa Chadwick?"

24

INTERRUPTING A PEACEFUL SCENE

It may have recently turned into a hotbed of crime, but Picklemarsh was rather beautiful. The rolling hills that encircled one side of the village were perfect for enjoying breathtaking views of the village, the valley, and beyond.

Not that they both were taking advantage of those views, no. Clara was, but Vanessa was studiously looking into each field they passed, clearly on the lookout for Pippa Chadwick.

"So, when you said we might bump into Pippa," Clara started, "you actually meant that you're going to actively seek her out if she's up here?"

"Of course," Vanessa replied. "It's a golden opportunity. Pippa may not know about Julian's death; we can evaluate her reaction. Or maybe Pippa knows something that she shouldn't know. In which case, we have a lead."

"You don't think Pippa did it, do you?" Clara asked, remembering the waif-like young girl and her naïve manner.

"You can never discount anyone," Vanessa reminded her.

"Appearances can be deceiving. But, even if Pippa didn't do it, that doesn't mean she can't know who did. Especially if the prime suspect is her boyfriend."

Clara didn't like the idea that Edward had jumped to the top of the list. Firstly, because she actually quite liked him. Secondly, because it didn't necessarily answer the question of who killed Angus Chadwick. And the idea of Picklemarsh having two murderers wasn't a pleasant one.

"Ah, there she is," Vanessa said. She pointed across the field to a large oak tree with overhanging branches that provided shade and shelter to the woman sitting below them.

Pippa Chadwick had a folding chair, an easel, and various painting supplies. It looked like a picture-perfect scene, one that Clara knew was about to be ruined by her aunt barging in and questioning the poor girl about a murder. A murder she probably hadn't heard about yet.

"Hello, my dear," Vanessa greeted Pippa, opening the field gate and waving.

Pippa turned and waved back. "Hi, Miss Harrington. Clara!"

They walked over to the tree, and Clara looked out to appreciate the view. She had to hand it to Pippa, she'd picked the perfect spot.

"It's beautiful up here," Clara whispered.

"Isn't it?" Pippa agreed. "I often come up here to just get away from everything." She placed her paintbrush on the easel's shelf and wiped her hands on a cloth. "Painting helps me take my mind off of things. Sometimes it's good to have a hobby, something that can just transport you."

Clara thought about her violin. She didn't play as much as she'd like, mainly because she knew the sound wasn't for everyone, but playing the stringed instrument was how she escaped from reality.

"Indeed it does," Vanessa said. "Especially needed in dark times like this, with two murders in such a short space of time."

Pippa spun to face Vanessa. "Two?"

Vanessa nodded. "I'm sorry, did you not hear?"

"Hear what?" Pippa demanded. "What's happened?"

"I'm afraid that Julian Bridgewater was murdered."

Clara watched Pippa's mouth drop open. She stared at Vanessa in shock before gradually looking away. Clara would stake money that Pippa hadn't known that—that or Pippa was an extremely good actress.

"Oh, how horrible," Pippa mumbled. "That's... that's..."

"Obviously your father and Julian worked together, but do you know of any particular business dealings they had lately? Something that might have upset someone enough to..." Vanessa trailed off.

Pippa shook her head. "Nothing I know of. My father wouldn't have spoken to me about business matters anyway. But he was head of the council, and Julian is an accountant for almost everyone in the village. Was. He was an accountant."

She turned back to her easel and started to gather her brushes. "I'm sorry, I need to get home. I didn't know Julian very well, but I'm not very good with death. It scares me so much."

She quickly packed her things away. As she did, Clara noted that her hands shook.

"It can be very unsettling," Vanessa agreed.

"I think I must have a phobia," Pippa said. "Death just… terrifies me. My mother had to sit with me for ages after my father died. The police had to prise us apart."

Vanessa raised an eyebrow towards Clara before turning back to Pippa. "So, just so I can understand the sequence of events, when your father died… what did you do?"

Pippa closed the travel box of paints and brushes and packed away her canvas. "I ran to my room. My mother followed me. I sat on my bed and cried. It was ridiculous, I didn't even like him, but just the thought of death had me in pieces."

"And you remained in your room until the police came?" Vanessa clarified.

"Yes, Inspector Ellis came up and separated us. I was in shock, I think." Pippa shook her head and picked up all of her various items. "I'm sorry, I feel rather sick. I need to get back home."

"Would you like us to walk with you?" Clara offered.

Pippa was already walking away as she shook her head. "No, thank you, though. I'm sorry. Bye!" Pippa hurried towards the gate and disappeared into the pathway.

"Well, that was interesting," Vanessa said. "Jemima Vos tells us that Genevieve stayed with Angus, and now Pippa tells us that Genevieve was with her. Someone is lying."

Clara nodded. "I'd like to say that maybe Pippa remembers incorrectly as she's obviously not good with death, but you'd remember whether or not your mother held you as you cried in your bedroom."

"Precisely. So, someone is lying. I'd like to know exactly where Genevieve Chadwick was after her husband was murdered, and I'd like to know who is lying about it, and why."

25

THE DROPPED PEN

Clara didn't think it was possible, but it had finally happened. She'd had enough of tea.

When they arrived home, Vanessa put the kettle on. Clara quickly shook her head and got herself a cold glass of water instead. She waited while Vanessa made herself a cup of tea, and then they both sat on their respective seats in the living room.

"Two murders," Clara mumbled.

"Indeed." Vanessa sipped her tea, her expression pensive.

"Do you think the same person killed Julian?" Clara asked. "Do you think Julian knew something, something about the murder of Angus? That ended up getting him killed, I mean."

"Possibly." Vanessa put her cup and saucer on the side table and looked seriously at Clara. "Do you want to go back to London? I know you left to have a break and relax. All of this clearly isn't very relaxing."

Clara shook her head. "I'm fine."

"Are you sure? I don't want to feel like you are staying

here if you don't want to. I know murders and investigations aren't at all why you came here."

It was true. If Clara could have chosen to have a break from London without two prominent members of the village being murdered, and without herself being dragged around questioning people, often illegally, she would have preferred it.

But the mystery of it all was eating at her. She wanted to know more, to understand. Every time she felt she had a slight understanding of what was happening, another thing happened, and she lost it again.

She never could have predicted a second murder, and while she had met people she didn't particularly like, she couldn't imagine accusing one of them of being a killer.

She wanted answers, though, and knew she wouldn't be able to rest until she got them.

"I'm okay," Clara repeated. "It's not a conventional holiday, but I'm certainly not bored. And it's taken my mind off my problems."

"As long as you're sure?" Vanessa asked.

Clara bit her lip. "As long as you don't mind me staying?"

Vanessa chuckled. "Mind? I want you to stay, I love having you here. I just want to make sure that you're okay. I'm meant to be offering you a quiet respite from London life."

Clara laughed. "Well, maybe things will calm down once we find out who the killers are."

"Indeed. If there's a third murder around here, then I'm afraid I'll have to move," Vanessa confessed. "After I solve the crime, of course."

"So, who do we question next?" Clara asked.

"We need to get to the bottom of this Genevieve mystery, and find out if and why Jemima lied. And then there's Felicity. Julian called her before he died. What was said? Why did he call her so late at night?"

Clara had been wondering the same thing. She itched to see Felicity again. She felt as if there was something between them, but, at the same time, she wanted to hold back for fear that she could be falling for a killer.

"I can go and see her," Clara suggested. "See what I can find out about the call. You know you're not always the most subtle, Aunt Vee."

Vanessa raised an eyebrow. "Neither are you, my dear."

Clara felt her cheeks heat. "I-I'm not sure what excuse to use, though. I don't want it to look like I'm just going to quiz her about the call."

Vanessa rolled her eyes. "You need to get creative, dear." She stood up and walked over to her desk. She rummaged in the pen pot for a couple of seconds before producing a plain black rollerball with a silver clip. "She dropped this when she was here. You're returning it."

Clara's eyes widened as she took the pen. "I can't do that, it's not hers."

"Well, of course it's not, but you can pretend that she dropped it. When she says it's not hers, you can say it must be someone else's and bring it back. In the meantime, you can talk to her." Vanessa sat down again. "I really thought I raised you to be sneakier."

"You raised me to be honest," Clara told her.

"More fool me."

26

MORE SNOOPING

Clara rode her bike towards the council office. Her heart was thundering in her chest, only in small part from the exertion of cycling. The rest was the prospect of seeing Felicity again.

She felt guilty for being happy on a day when someone had been murdered. She hardly knew Julian, but she felt like she should keep smiling to a minimum. Surely the village was in mourning?

The few people she had passed while out seemed to be acting normal enough, but then there was the chance that the news hadn't spread yet.

Although that seemed highly unlikely, especially in a place as small as Picklemarsh, and this being the second murder within a week.

Clara pulled up outside of the council office and chained her bike to the railing. She smiled to herself. If she did that anywhere in London, then the chain would be cut and the bike taken away within minutes. It was a very different world out here in the country.

She walked into the offices, her hand in her pocket

clutching at the pen, her supposed excuse for coming. It felt childish to need an excuse to see Felicity, but the pen was a great security blanket.

Clara was just coming up with something to say to the receptionist when Felicity entered reception with a handful of papers, issuing instructions to someone who walked beside her.

Clara stopped dead and looked at her, unable to tear her eyes away.

Felicity must have felt that she was being watched and looked up to meet Clara's gaze. She smiled, handed the paperwork to her colleague, and approached.

"Hello, Clara. To what do I owe the pleasure?"

Clara took the pen out of her pocket and held it out.

"I… found this. At my aunt's house. We think it might be yours?"

If Felicity saw through the flimsy subterfuge, she didn't make it obvious. She took the pen from Clara's shaking hand and regarded it for a moment.

"No, this isn't mine, but thank you for coming all the way over here to drop it off in case it was." Felicity handed it back. "Can I offer you a drink?"

Clara looked at the receptionist who had been watching their interaction and wondered if the woman had seen right through her.

"I'd like that, thank you." Clara pocketed the pen.

Felicity gestured towards the stairs. They walked up to Felicity's office, and Clara took a seat in front of her desk.

"Tea? Coffee?" Felicity offered.

Clara made a face. "Just water, please."

Felicity raised an eyebrow.

"I've drunk about twenty cups of tea a day since living with my aunt," Clara admitted. "I'm bouncing off the walls."

Felicity chuckled. "Yes, I do recall staying with older relatives in my youth. The kettle was on every twenty to thirty minutes."

"Exactly."

Felicity walked over to the drinks table and picked up the empty jug. "I'll be back in a moment. I'll just go and get a refill."

After she left, Clara looked around the room, knowing that Aunt Vee would most certainly use the opportunity to snoop around. She wondered if she should. But her heart was beating out of her chest and she thought if she were caught, she would surely have a heart attack there and then.

She did look at the desk, realising for the first time that she absolutely couldn't read upside down. There was a memo with a pen resting on it. Clara focused on it and started to tilt her head.

"It's a memo from me to the hitman I hired to kill Julian," Felicity announced when she came back into the room with two glasses of water. "You got me."

Clara sat back in her chair and shook her head. "I... I wasn't snooping."

"You just came to see me on the day Julian was murdered to hand back a pen?" Felicity asked, but she was smiling.

"I... yes," Clara agreed.

"You really are terrible at lying," Felicity informed her as she took her seat. She put her glass of water down, picked up the memo, and turned it to show Clara. "Complaining about the cost of tree maintenance in the area, nothing interesting."

Clara glanced at the memo, confirming it was what Felicity claimed. She could feel the blush on her cheeks at being so obvious.

"So, did you kill Julian?" she asked cheekily. She thought she might as well just come out and ask considering that's what Felicity thought she was there for.

Felicity put the memo back on her desk. "No, I didn't kill Julian. Nor Angus. Nor indeed anyone." She pointed to the empty chair next to Clara. "Is your aunt not with you today?"

"We're not joined at the hip," Clara said, although she had to admit she'd rarely been separated from her aunt since she arrived in Picklemarsh. When she had been, she'd nearly been hit by a car.

Felicity held up her hands. "I'm sorry, I didn't realise that was a sore point."

Clara let out a sigh. "No, I'm sorry. I… this has all been a little hard. I don't want to come and ask you if you murdered someone, but you *are* a suspect."

"I am," Felicity agreed. "But I can't do much more than assure you that I didn't do it."

"I know about the phone call," Clara confessed. "Made from Julian to you last night."

"Yes, I was out. He left a voicemail," Felicity explained. "He didn't say a lot. The police have taken a recording of it."

Clara's eyebrows knitted together. The call was made quite late at night, at nearly eleven. She knew it was none of her business, but she had to ask. "Where were you?"

Felicity leaned back in her chair. "I went out for a drive

to clear my mind, what with everything that has been happening around here lately."

Clara swallowed. As flimsy excuses went, it was up there.

"When I got back, I didn't even notice I had a voicemail from Julian. I went straight to bed. The next morning the police arrived." Felicity gestured around the room. "But I'm here, so they clearly don't think I did it."

Clara considered that maybe they didn't have enough evidence to arrest her yet, but she didn't want to say that. She hadn't come here to be confrontational. She came to gather information in hopes that Felicity could provide her with some cast-iron alibi so that Clara wouldn't have to constantly flip-flop between being attracted to the woman and wondering if she was a killer.

"I'm sorry I can't tell you anything more concrete," Felicity said, seemingly detecting Clara's distress. "No one wishes I had a better excuse than I do, believe me."

Clara picked up the glass and took a sip of water. She wasn't thirsty, it was just to bide her time. To spend longer in Felicity's presence and think about what to say next.

"I just want some answers," Clara admitted, placing the glass down.

"A lot of people do," Felicity agreed.

"Was there anything strange about the night of Angus' murder?" Clara asked, desperately hoping for a grain of new information that might just crack the case wide open.

"It was all strange," Felicity admitted. "I argued with Angus, but to be honest there was nothing strange about that."

"What did you argue about?"

"Work. We always argued about work. Angus couldn't

separate his personal life from work. If he had a disagreement with someone, he often wanted to use his council powers to penalise them in some way. It was often up to me to stop him."

Clara nodded. That matched up with what she had heard about the man. She was glad that Felicity managed to rein him in.

"He also argued bitterly with Sylvester King. I saw him come storming out of Angus' office after raised voices were heard." Felicity let out a sigh. "But, as I said to the police, arguing with Angus was normal for everyone. He wasn't a very easy person to be around. Raised voices and threats were a day-to-day occurrence for him."

Clara scrunched up her face, deep in thought. She wondered what else Aunt Vee might ask. She really wasn't much good at this investigation malarkey at all.

"Are you seeing anyone?" Felicity suddenly asked.

Clara blinked. "Um. No. No, I'm not."

"Maybe, if you'd like, we could go for a drink one night?" Felicity said, nerves obvious in her tone.

Clara felt her eyes open wide. "Yes! I mean, yes, I'd like that."

Felicity smiled. "Good, I'd hoped I hadn't misread the signals. Or your aunt's very obvious matchmaking."

Clara groaned. "I'm sorry about her."

"Don't be," Felicity said. "I probably would never have asked if she hadn't meddled."

Clara chuckled and rolled her eyes. "Great, now I'll have to tell her she was right."

Felicity handed her mobile over to Clara. "May I have your number? I'll contact you when things have died down a little." She winced. "Poor choice of words. You know what I mean."

Clara took the phone and nodded. She quickly added her mobile number, noting the way her hands softly shook. She was going on a date with Felicity Abbot. She couldn't believe it.

She handed the phone back. "I look forward to it."

27

THE PERFECT LOCATION

Clara unlocked her bike and walked away from the council offices with a wide grin on her face. She may have been no closer to knowing if Felicity was a killer or not, but she had a date with her.

She needed to get home and speak to Aunt Vee. Her aunt had seemed to have some thoughts on who Angus' murderer was. Hopefully she'd be able to crack the case, prove Felicity innocent, and then Clara could get on with her life.

She got onto her bike and started to ride down the road. The Milton Furnishings shop was being emptied, and she let out a sigh. She wondered how many other people would find their finances mismanaged by Julian and have to move or go out of business as a result.

Mrs Milton exited the shop, and Clara slowed to a stop.

"Hello again, dear," Mrs Milton greeted her.

"Hi. I'm sorry to hear you're closing down," Clara said.

"So am I," Mrs Milton agreed. "I'll miss this place. Still, maybe someone will make a better go of it than we were able

185

to. Looks like it might be an estate agency, which is a shame."

Clara nodded. "Yes, it does seem like a waste of a good spot on the high street."

"I thought Anton Vos would snap it up," Mrs Milton said.

"Why?"

"For the farm shop. They do very well, and it's grown a lot over the last few years. But they are so far out of the way. A central shop in the high street would be perfect for them. Would stop Alf from having the monopoly as well. I often saw Jemima in the shop, but she didn't look like she was browsing for furniture, if you know what I mean?"

"More like she was deciding where to put hers?" Clara asked.

"Exactly. But we heard that an estate agency has snapped up the lease. Shame for the high street."

"Janet? Can you help me with this?" Mr Milton called from inside the shop.

"I better go," Mrs Milton said.

"Yes, me too," Clara said. "Good luck!"

Mrs Milton waved her goodbye as Clara pushed off on her bike and continued on her way home.

She turned the corner and could smell something odd in the air. She stopped for a second and looked around to see if she could discover where it was coming from. A few seconds later she saw a small plume of black smoke coming from behind a cottage.

Cycling closer, she stopped by the wall and lifted herself up to have a look over. She told herself that she was just checking that people were okay, not actually spying on anyone.

In the back garden of the cottage she saw Sylvester King. He was throwing handfuls of paper into a large metal barbeque.

Clara looked around to see if anyone was around, but the road was completely empty. She bit her lip, wondering what on earth Sylvester was doing. Was he just clearing out old papers? Was he paranoid about identity theft?

She had no idea.

Whatever it was, she didn't like it. She climbed down from the wall and got back on her bike. Sylvester King had every right to burn papers in his own back garden, but that didn't mean she wouldn't be telling Aunt Vee about it.

She'd had a very successful afternoon of investigation. Perhaps she was better at this than she thought.

"Hmm, very interesting," Vanessa said. "On the day of Julian's death, no less."

Clara nodded. "Yes, that's what I thought. I would have thought basic common sense would have told someone not to burn things in their back garden just after a murder. Possibly double murder."

"Never been one for common sense, that man," Vanessa explained. "Did you hear about the gathering?"

Clara shook her head.

"The community decided that we should have a gathering in two days' time, to pay respects to those who are no longer with us. It will be at the church."

"Oh, yes, that seems like a good idea," Clara agreed.

"It does," Vanessa said. "And a great opportunity to see all of our suspects in one room at the same time. If they all decide to attend, that is. It would look extremely suspicious if anyone decided not to go."

"Surely, it's about paying respects to the dead, not trying to look innocent?" Clara said.

"Well, some will no doubt try to do both." Vanessa walked over to a bookcase and picked up a plastic bag from one of the shelves. She took out a knitting project and returned to the sofa.

"I spoke to Janet Milton. She said that an estate agency is moving into the old Milton Furnishings shop," Clara said.

Vanessa scrunched up her face. "Why?"

"I don't know, just passing on the message."

Vanessa shook her head. "Such a lovely location, that's a waste."

"Mrs Milton agreed. She had thought that Vos Farm might take the shop. Apparently, Jemima Vos had been in there a few times, scouting." Clara picked up her phone and opened up the news app, deciding to see what was happening in the outside world.

"It would be a good location for them. I wonder why they didn't take it?" Vanessa asked.

"Too expensive?" Clara suggested.

"Possibly."

"There's something else," Clara said, keeping her eyes fixed on her phone so as not to show her nerves.

"Felicity Abbot asked you out?" Vanessa guessed.

Clara stared at her. "How on earth could you know that?"

"You're smiling, you keep checking your phone, you didn't say a word about your discussion with her, but you immediately mentioned Sylvester, and she looked at you as if she wanted to ask you out when she was here. Doesn't take a mind reader, dear."

Clara put her phone face down on the sofa beside her and folded her arms. "Well, if it's all that obvious, I don't see how you haven't solved the case already."

"Not everyone is as transparent as you," Vanessa told her.

"Should I go?"

"Out with Felicity?"

"Yes."

Vanessa looked thoughtfully out of the window for a moment. "Maybe wait a few days."

"What's going to happen in a few days?"

"We'll see," Vanessa said. "It just seems to me that all of this is coming to a head."

Clara let out a breath and slumped into the sofa. She knew it was wise to wait. Felicity had said so herself. That didn't mean she liked it. This kind of thing never happened to her, the woman she crushed on asking her out. She wanted to grab the opportunity, even if it did scare her.

She picked up her phone again and tried to focus on catching up with world events. For once, they seemed to pale in comparison to what was happening locally.

28

AN ARREST

Alf Higginbottom was practically vibrating with excitement when they stopped into the greengrocer's the next morning. Clara had barely picked up a shopping basket when he dashed around the counter and made a beeline for Vanessa.

"Have you heard?" he asked, in a tone that indicated he knew she hadn't.

Vanessa looked at the display of cakes. "That you're finally discounting these pre-packaged monstrosities that are about to go off?"

He ignored the comment. "About Pippa Chadwick and Edward Milton."

Vanessa frowned. "What about them?"

"Arrested." Alf nodded his head. "Last night. Trying to leave the village in the middle of the night, someone saw them and called it in. The police arrested them. All very suspicious, if you ask me."

Clara wanted to mention that they hadn't asked him but knew that wasn't the best way to garner more information from the man.

"How do you know about this?" Vanessa asked.

"Mrs Sackville, they were stopped outside her house. She had the window open for some air and heard the whole thing. Inspector Ellis arrested them on the suspicion of murder, both Angus Chadwick and Julian Bridgewater." Alf folded his arms in a 'what do you say about that' kind of manner.

Vanessa tilted her head to the side as she seemed to consider the matter. Then she shook her head.

"Edward, maybe. But Pippa, I think not," she decided.

"They were running away in the middle of the night. Pretty conclusive, if you ask me."

"I think if I were her, and my father had been murdered, I might consider running away," Clara pointed out. "Especially if a second murder occurred not long after."

"Mrs Sackville heard it?" Vanessa asked.

"Yes, they were coming down from Upper Lane, that's where they were stopped."

Vanessa turned to say something to Clara but looked over her shoulder and narrowed her eyes.

"Interesting," she murmured.

Clara turned to see Sylvester King through the shop window. He was on the other side of the street, walking in the opposite direction.

"You know, I think I've forgotten my shopping list," Vanessa announced. She peeked into her handbag for a moment. "Yes, I have. We'll have to come back later. Come on, Clara."

Vanessa was already out of the shop by the time Clara lowered the basket and said a hurried goodbye to Alf.

"Come on, let's not dawdle," Vanessa said, hurrying along the street in the opposite direction to the one Sylvester was travelling.

Clara rushed to catch up. "Where are we going?"

"Sylvester's house," Vanessa explained. "You said he was burning papers yesterday, and we now know he's out of the house. There may be something left behind. We can't let the opportunity go to waste."

Clara mentally added breaking and entering to the list of crimes and lies that Vanessa was more than happy to undertake as part of her not quite legal investigation.

"Can we do that?" she asked.

"We'll find out."

"I mean legally, should we?"

"I'm not going to call Inspector Ellis to find out," Vanessa said. "Besides, he's too busy interviewing Pippa and Edward, I'm sure."

"Do you think they did it?"

"Unlikely. I think they naively decided to leave, and someone reported them for it. The thing is, if someone was travelling from Chadwick Manor down Upper Lane, there's only really one person who could see them and report them."

Clara looked around the roads to get her bearings, trying to recall which road was which.

"Sylvester King," Vanessa explained. "His window looks out at the lane. No one else could see them."

"So, yesterday he was burning paperwork, and last night he called the police on Pippa and Edward."

"Exactly, which might mean he thought they were

running away, or might mean he is trying to distract the police."

They hurried down the street, nodding politely to the people that they passed. Before long they came to Sylvester's cottage. Vanessa reached over the gate and unlocked it and walked in.

Clara paused on the other side, not sure if she wanted to enter the garden.

"Should one of us be a lookout?" she asked.

"Only if you want us to look extremely suspicious," Vanessa told her. "Act with confidence, we're meant to be here. Come on."

Vanessa turned on her heel and walked around the cottage and into the back garden. Clara looked around the street one last time before she followed, carefully closing the gate behind her as she did.

When she got to the back garden, Vanessa was already examining the sooty remains in the barbeque. Clara looked into the metal container and sighed. It looked like most of the paperwork was completely destroyed. The odd small fragment that had survived was blank.

"Nothing," she muttered.

"Indeed. Oh well, it was worth checking. If it was worth burning, then it was worth seeing if any of it remained." Vanessa continued to poke at the charred remains.

Clara looked around the garden. She felt a chill at trespassing. She kept expecting Sylvester to appear out of nowhere, catching them in the act. He'd probably call the police on them. He'd be perfectly within his rights.

Something caught her eye, and she gasped. She crouched

down behind a large flowerpot and stared in horror at the house.

"What is it?" Vanessa asked.

"Someone's in the house," Clara told her. "Get down!"

Vanessa took a few steps and stood behind a tree, peering at the house.

"The window on the right. I saw someone, I'm sure of it," Clara said.

She was about to suggest that they sneak around the other side of the cottage and get out of the garden as soon as possible, when Vanessa did the unthinkable. She started to creep towards the house.

Clara couldn't do anything. If she moved, she may draw attention to them. If she called for Aunt Vee, there'd be the same result. So, she simply watched in horror as Vanessa approached the house in a slow crouch that did absolutely nothing to hide her presence.

"I'm going to prison," Clara muttered to herself.

Vanessa got to the house and slowly stood up, looking in through the window. Clara's heart was in her mouth. Vanessa looked through the window for a few seconds before turning and gesturing for Clara to join her by the side of the house.

Clara swallowed hard and then made a beeline for her aunt. When she got close, Vanessa tilted her head towards the side of the house and the exit.

"They've gone upstairs, let's go," Vanessa said.

Clara wasn't about to argue. They crept around the house, back to the gate they'd entered through, and out into the street. The relief Clara felt was immense.

"Never do that again," she pleaded.

"But if we hadn't then we wouldn't have the information we now have," Vanessa said.

"All the paperwork was destroyed," Clara pointed out.

"It was. But if we hadn't checked, then we wouldn't have seen Genevieve Chadwick in Sylvester King's house."

29

A FINGERPRINT MATCH

They hurried away from Sylvester King's house and back towards the high street. Vanessa was deep in thought, and Clara was too busy panicking to question her.

Instead, she wondered to herself if Genevieve had seen them. More importantly, why was Genevieve in Sylvester's house? And of even greater importance than that, was she supposed to be there?

A car slowed beside them, and Clara stopped when she saw it was Will Ellis.

"Good morning," he greeted them through the open driver's window.

Clara was too surprised to speak, worried that he was about to arrest them for trespass. How had he gotten there so quickly? Or was he simply following them and waiting for them to break the law? Again?

"I hear you made an arrest, Inspector?" Vanessa said. "Or should I say, two arrests?"

Will chuckled. "Word spreads quickly around here, don't they?"

"They do," Vanessa agreed. "Do you have any actual evidence to hold them?"

Will drummed his fingers on the steering wheel and looked straight ahead. "We're still investigating." He let out a sigh. He turned to face them. "We don't have anything yet. We'll have to let them go soon. But you have to admit, it is very suspicious to be leaving town at the moment. Especially in the middle of the night."

"Suspicious, but not unheard of," Vanessa replied.

Will shrugged a shoulder. "We'll see." His mobile phone rang, and he tapped the hands-free earpiece he wore. "Ellis?"

Vanessa took a step closer, not at all worried about listening in on a private conversation. Probably hoping that she could, more like.

Clara looked around the street, noting that they were getting a few sideways glances from people. She couldn't blame them. Two murders, a selection of potential suspects. If this was her home, she'd want to know what was happening as well.

"I see. I'm nearby, I'll pick her up now," Will said.

Clara's heartrate spiked. Had he just been informed of their presence in Sylvester King's garden? Were they about to be arrested?

Will hung up his call and sighed.

"News, Inspector?" Vanessa asked, completely unperturbed at the fact they may soon be joining Pippa and Edward in lock-up.

"The results on the cocktail glass you found in the fireplace in Angus Chadwick's study have just come in," he explained. "Two sets of fingerprints were found. Angus Chadwick... and Felicity Abbot."

Clara swallowed hard.

"I see," Vanessa said.

Will parked the car and got out. He walked towards the council offices, Vanessa in hot pursuit.

"What happens now?" she asked.

"I have to arrest her on suspicion of murder," Will said.

"What? You can't," Clara told him. "She—you don't have enough evidence."

"I'm afraid I do," Will said. "She was at the house that night, has a motive, no alibi, and the fingerprint evidence is the icing on the cake."

He pushed opened the door to the council office, got his ID out of his pocket, and showed it to the receptionist.

"I need to speak to Felicity Abbot. Is she in?" he asked.

The receptionist shook her head, looking from Will to Vanessa and then to Clara. "No, she's working from home today."

"Thank you." Will turned around and edged past Vanessa and Clara.

Clara looked pleadingly at Vanessa, but she sadly shook her head. "I'm sorry, there's not a lot we can do."

"She's innocent," Clara whispered. "We have to prove it."

"Come on." Vanessa dragged her by the arm out of the council office. When they were outside, she called out to Will.

He paused by the car and looked at her with a questioning frown.

"We're coming, too," Vanessa informed him.

He looked like he was about to argue but quickly gave up, probably realising that it was the path of least resistance.

"Fine, fine, hurry up," he said, opening the back passenger door and gesturing for them to get in.

They arrived at Felicity's house in a couple of minutes. Clara's mouth was dry; she couldn't believe this was happening. She'd gone from not knowing if Felicity was innocent to absolute certainty that she must be. She didn't know why she was now so sure, especially in the face of actual evidence that she may well not be.

Will got out of the car, and Vanessa hurried after him. Clara trailed behind, half wanting to be there and half wanting to not be.

"If you interfere with this arrest, I'll have no choice but to arrest you as well," Will informed Vanessa.

"I have no intention of interfering. I'm merely investigating. I don't believe you have enough evidence to properly convict Miss Abbot," Vanessa said. "I'll either help you find more evidence or prove her innocence. A win-win for you, surely."

Will didn't say anything. He hammered on the front door, a determined look on his face.

A minute went by, and then Felicity opened the door. She looked confused by the three of them standing outside.

"Felicity Abbot, you are under arrest," Will announced.

Felicity's jaw actually dropped open. She looked at Clara and then back to Will.

"On what charges?" she breathed.

"I'm arresting you for the murder of Angus Chadwick," Will said. "You do not have to say anything, but it may harm your defence if you do not mention when questioned something which you later rely on in court…"

Clara tuned out the rest of his speech. She'd heard it on television a hundred times before. Instead, she looked at Felicity who looked to be in utter shock.

"I didn't do it," she said.

Vanessa put a hand on her arm. "Just go with Inspector Ellis. You can sort everything out at the station."

Felicity looked at Clara. "I didn't do this," she assured her.

"Will you come with me, please?" The inspector gestured towards the car.

"Go," Vanessa encouraged her. "We'll make sure there is food and water down for your cat."

Felicity looked at Vanessa for a second before nodding. She gestured towards a hook on the wall. "There's a spare key there. Lock up when you're done." She picked up her handbag and nodded to Will that she was ready to leave.

Clara watched them walk down the path. Will opened the back door of the car and waited for Felicity to get in. He closed the door behind her, nodded towards Clara and Vanessa, and a few moments later he was gone.

Clara wanted to cry; such was the emotion building up inside her. Things were moving too fast. For the first time in a while she wished she were back in London.

"Come on, let's see what we can find." Vanessa wrapped an arm around her waist and guided her into the house.

Once they were inside, Clara closed the door and Vanessa immediately started snooping.

It wasn't long before they found a small downstairs study. It was neater than Angus' or even Julian's, and Clara smiled at the differences. This room was warm, cosy, well-ordered, and even smelt good.

Vanessa didn't seem interested in the furnishings as she flipped through paperwork in the in tray.

"Look at this." She pulled out several documents. "Core Foods has been repeatedly denied planning permission. Felicity was instructing environmental impact reports on their proposed building. She managed to block it at every turn."

"That wouldn't have made her popular," Clara said.

"No, it really wouldn't." Vanessa put the papers back. She looked around the desk, reading the various other pieces of paper she found.

Clara turned and examined the rest of the room. There was a small sofa with a welcoming cushion on it. She sat down and looked at her aunt rummaging through desk drawers.

In another life she could imagine herself sitting there, reading a book while Felicity worked into the night. She swallowed, not realising how invested she had become in a possible relationship until it was taken away from her.

When had she really fallen for Felicity?

"Is that the answerphone?" Vanessa asked, pointing to the table beside the sofa.

Clara leaned over the arm. "Yes. Old school, I thought everyone had gone digital these days."

"Welcome to Picklemarsh," Vanessa said.

"Should I press play?" Clara asked.

"Absolutely."

She pressed the button, and the machine whirred into life, playing the last received message.

"Felicity, it's Julian. I've gotten your letter, and this is really petty. Even for you. There is no reason for planning permission to be denied yet again. You need to do your job and get that paperwork sorted out. Now."

Clara blinked. The animosity in the tone was clear. Julian was livid.

"Play that again," Vanessa requested.

Clara hit the play button. The message played again. Vanessa stood up and walked closer to the machine, leaning down to put her ear closer to the speaker.

"Again," she said.

Clara pressed the button again.

Vanessa leaned even closer, closing her eyes and listening.

"Hmm." She stood up. "Interesting."

"What's interesting?" Clara asked.

"Can you access this laptop? It seems to be on and unlocked." Vanessa pointed to the desk.

Clara sighed, realising she wasn't going to get an answer to her question. She stood up and walked around the desk and took Felicity's chair. She wiggled the mouse and pulled the laptop closer to her.

"Okay, what do you want to look at?" she asked.

"Emails. Let's start with the night of the murder." Vanessa stood behind her, leaning on the high-backed chair and looking at the screen.

"Nothing," Clara said. She scrolled up and down. "It's weird. There's... nothing there for that day. Every other day there are loads of emails."

"Could they have been deleted?"

Clara checked the trash folder and nodded. "Yes, here

they are. She received an email from Angus Chadwick at half past six. That's just before the dinner."

Clara opened the email, and they both sucked in a breath.

"Well, that's Angus Chadwick for you," Vanessa said.

"'I'll kill you,'" Clara read. "He's actually threatening to kill Felicity."

She shook her head, unable to believe what she was reading. What kind of person said such things?

"Maybe she decided to get there first?" Vanessa wondered.

"Aunt Vee!"

"And then deleted the emails as they pointed to a motive," Vanessa continued.

"Or she knew they looked inflammatory so that was why she deleted them," Clara suggested.

"What led up to that threat?" Vanessa asked.

Clara scrolled through the email. There was a very long thread of back-and-forth messages, predominantly about paperwork and planning permission. Angus was furious with Felicity, and Felicity was not best pleased with him.

Vanessa pointed to the screen. "There it is again, another threat to kill her. Seems Angus liked to threaten people with murder."

"He climbs down in his next paragraph," Clara stated. "Apologising. As if that fixes everything."

"They had a very fiery relationship."

"It's not evidence of murder," Clara said.

"No, but it's more motive. The police will no doubt be applying for a warrant to search this laptop. It doesn't look good."

"It's not that cut and dry," Clara said. "Surely?"

"Maybe this explains why she was late to dinner that night?" Vanessa considered. "She'd just had a terrible back-and-forth email conversation with Angus and was considering not showing up as a result."

"I wish she hadn't."

"I'm sure she wishes the same." Vanessa took a step back. "Come on, let's go."

Clara frowned. "Don't you want to go through the rest of the laptop?"

Vanessa shook her head. "No, I think I have all I need."

"Should we feed the cat?" Clara asked.

Vanessa laughed. "There is no cat, darling."

Clara slumped in the chair, annoyed at herself for being had yet again.

30

THE FINAL PIECES

Clara watched the raindrops sliding down the window. She'd been sitting by the window for the last hour, cuddled up in a soft blanket, watching the heavens open to soak the back garden of Chadwick Lodge.

They'd been home for a few hours, and Vanessa had been writing all that time.

It suited Clara perfectly; she wasn't in the mood to talk. She wished she'd done more when Felicity had been arrested, not that there was anything she could have done. It was hard to feel so useless, though, watching as she was taken away.

And still the question lingered: was she guilty?

Vanessa had continued to claim that she didn't know. Clara thought her aunt knew more than she was letting on. She'd be surprised if her aunt's astute brain hadn't at least put most of it together by now.

A knock on the door made her jump.

"I'll go," she said. "But if it's Will Ellis come to arrest us for trespass…"

"I keep telling you," Vanessa replied, "my hat blew into the garden."

"You don't have a hat."

"Because it blew away."

Clara rolled her eyes and opened the door. She blinked a few times at the sight of Pippa Chadwick and Edward Milton standing on the porch. They both had their wax jackets held over their heads to protect them from the rain.

"Hi…" she greeted them.

"Hey," Edward said. "Can we come in? We'd like to speak to your aunt."

Clara realised she was blocking the path for no good reason and let them in. She took their coats and hung them on hooks above the radiator where they could dry out.

"Aunt Vee, it's Pippa and Edward," she announced, gesturing for them to go straight through to the back room.

When she joined them, Vanessa had stood up and smiled to greet them. "Hello. Do sit down, you two."

Edward and Pippa sat down on the sofa, butted up against one another and looking very small and very lost.

"We didn't do it," Edward said first.

Vanessa sat on the sofa opposite. "Well, it seems the police let you go. That's a good start."

"Only because they say they don't have enough evidence," Pippa said. "I think they still think we did it."

"Which we didn't," Edward added.

"Which we didn't," Pippa agreed.

Clara took a seat next to Vanessa. "I don't mean to be rude, but why are you here?"

"Well, we know that you"—Pippa gestured to Vanessa

—"are a crime writer. Which makes you more qualified than either of us. We want your help to prove our innocence."

Vanessa raised her eyebrows. "I'm afraid that isn't really my area. I think you need a solicitor."

Pippa nodded. "We do. But a solicitor is going to try to get us out of a legal mess, not find the real killer. We didn't kill anyone, not my father or Julian Bridgewater. We thought maybe you could help us find out who did. Then the police would have the killer or killers and we could get on with our lives."

"Why were you running away?" Clara asked.

Pippa bit her lip and looked down in shame.

Edward held her hand. "Pippa didn't feel safe. Neither of us did, but especially not Pippa. Two people she knew well had been killed. We worried one of us would be next. We didn't tell anyone we were leaving because we worried the killer might find out. We just wanted to go."

"But someone saw you," Vanessa said.

"Yes, I thought we were being quiet and clever going in the middle of the night, but I see now how that must have looked very suspicious," he said.

"You weren't to know," Pippa reassured him.

"So, you didn't tell anyone that you were leaving? No one at all?" Vanessa asked.

Pippa shook her head. "No one. Well…"

"Well?" Vanessa queried.

"Jemima Vos was kind of the person who suggested it," Pippa confessed.

"How so?"

"She told me that if she was in my shoes, she'd leave. She

said you really didn't know who might be next. But she didn't know we'd actually do it. No one did."

"Not even your mother?" Vanessa pressed.

Pippa bit her lip. "No. I..." She trailed off, clearly unwilling to say anymore.

Clara and Vanessa exchanged a look.

"You?" Vanessa asked.

The turmoil in Pippa's eyes was crystal clear.

"If you want me to help you, I need to know everything. Even if you feel it incriminates someone else," Vanessa told her softly.

"I don't... trust her," Pippa confessed quietly. "She didn't seem upset when Father died. I know she didn't love him anymore, but she... she didn't even seem surprised. At first, I thought it was shock, but now I don't know."

"Tell her what you found," Edward said.

Pippa nodded and sucked in a quick breath. "The day after my father died, I was in my mother's room—they had separate rooms, you see. We often share lotions and make-up, that kind of thing, like mothers and daughters do."

Vanessa nodded her understanding.

"I saw this... this glass vial. It looked out of place. It was small, it had a glass and rubber stopper on the top of it. But no label. At first, I thought it was perfume, but my mother is very particular with perfume because she has allergies." She shrugged. "I didn't say or do anything, and a day later it was gone. Now I worry that was the poison."

"Did you tell anyone else you saw it?" Clara asked.

Pippa shook her head. "Only Edward."

"I think you need to tell Inspector Ellis," Vanessa said.

Pippa shook her head again. "I can't. What if it was

nothing? Or what if it was the poison, and Mother did kill him? Then she'd be angry with me."

Clara felt sorry for Pippa. She'd obviously been carrying this question around for a while and was tied up in knots about the right thing to do. No wonder she'd decided to run away.

"So, neither of you mentioned this glass vial while you were being questioned?" Vanessa asked.

"No," Pippa said.

"No. Though they questioned me relentlessly about the chemicals I use when I upcycle furniture," Edward said.

"They did the same to me," Pippa said. "Asked what kind of chemicals Edward uses, as if I'd know that."

"Do you use any chemicals that could be poisonous?" Vanessa asked.

Edward nodded. "Yeah, sure, but no one would drink any of it, not willingly."

Vanessa leaned back. "You say they were questioning you relentlessly?"

Edward nodded. "They wouldn't let up for a second."

"I think they were trying to exhaust you into a confession. Or perhaps convince Pippa that you might have done it, have her slip up and give them some information. It sounds like they didn't really have anything on either of you."

"But we do appear to be their number one suspects," Edward pointed out.

"Yes, it does seem that way."

Clara realised that the two had no idea Felicity had been arrested, and it seemed that Vanessa wasn't about to tell them.

"Have either of you spoken with Sylvester King?" Vanessa asked.

Pippa shook her head and made a repulsed face at the thought. Edward looked sheepish.

"Edward?" Pippa asked her boyfriend. "Why have you been talking to that awful old man?"

Edward turned to face Pippa head on. He held her hands. "Please don't be angry," he started.

Vanessa looked at Clara and raised her eyebrow.

"It was weeks ago. Your father had just sent my father a letter about putting his furniture outside his shop." Edward looked at Clara. "Which he is allowed to do, but Angus changed the law to prevent it. It was after that; I was in the pub and Sylvester got talking to me. I… I just wanted to teach Angus a lesson. So, I told Sylvester some stuff that I'd overheard. I knew it would go in his book, and it would annoy Angus. I'm sorry, I shouldn't have done it."

Pippa wrenched her hands out of his. "I can't believe you did that!"

"I'm sorry, I—"

"Stuff you'd overheard. You mean things I'd told you in confidence, right?"

Edward lowered his head and slowly nodded.

"I can't believe you!" Pippa huffed. "We're supposed to tell each other everything."

"Well, I think you can have this conversation elsewhere," Vanessa said, standing up.

Edward looked up at her, panic in his eyes. "But… can you help us?"

"Come to the church memorial tomorrow," she said.

Pippa looked up at her. "Why?"

"Because everyone will be there, and I have a feeling that all will come out tomorrow." Vanessa shooed them out of the room. "Go on, go. I'll see you tomorrow at the church."

The pair quickly put on their boots and coats and left, offering Clara a quick, questioning glance. She simply shrugged. She didn't know what Vanessa was thinking either.

The front door closed, and Clara leaned on the door-frame and folded her arms.

"All will come out tomorrow?" she asked.

Vanessa looked deep in thought. "Yes. It's all rather simple when you consider it."

"Are you going to explain it to me?" Clara asked.

Aunt Vee shook her head. "No, I'm going to sleep on it. Make sure I've covered every angle."

Clara knew she wouldn't be swayed. Once her aunt had made her mind up, that was that. As much as she was dying to know who Vanessa thought the murderer was, Clara was more relieved that the mystery had apparently been solved.

"Felicity?" she asked softly.

Vanessa offered her a warm smile. "Don't worry."

31

THE MEMORIAL... AND THE ANSWERS

The next morning Clara rose bright and early and put on a smart, light grey skirt, a white blouse, and a dark blazer. She didn't really know what to wear to a memorial in a small village, where two prominent men had been murdered, but she surmised smart and respectful was the way to go.

Vanessa had left early, leaving a note for Clara to meet her at the church at nine o'clock. Clara wondered what she was up to. She'd heard her walking around the house early in the morning but had left her to her pacing.

She remembered when she was younger and her aunt was dealing with a complex plot point. Aunt Vee would often go through a period where she slept strange hours and then spent her waking hours pacing in a dreamlike state.

It was all part of the process, Clara assumed.

She had a light breakfast and then walked to the church, which stood at the end of the high street. Everyone else seemed to be gathering as well, just like Vanessa had suggested they would.

Clara hoped a few were there to actually pay their

respects, but judging by how unpopular the men were, she supposed those numbers would be scarce.

She stepped inside the building and found herself immediately in the nave of the small country church. In front of her were rows of pews on each side of a central pathway and a small, raised altar at the other end of the nave.

She saw Vanessa in the very back row and edged along the benches to sit beside her. Clara could see all the key players in the murder case, as well as everyone else she'd met in the town since she'd arrived. There were plenty of new faces, too. Everyone was looking around, eager to see who else had arrived. Heads were bent together, and the murmurs of soft whispers filled the air.

A vicar arrived, and people started to take their seats and quieten down.

"Father Langford," Vanessa explained, directing her head towards the man who was approaching the stage.

Clara was watching the man when someone else caught her eye on the opposite row of benches.

"Is that Felicity?" she asked, her voice just a whisper.

Vanessa looked to the other side of the row. "Yes. Inspector Ellis let her attend."

"Dearly beloved," Father Langford began, "we're gathered here today to remember those who have recently departed this mortal coil."

Vanessa let out a breath of frustration. Clara elbowed her and shushed her. If they were going to attend a memorial service, then they were going to be polite about it.

Father Langford continued his speech. In a way so typical of a religious man, he glossed over the negative aspects of both men and focused on the good. He was deliberate in his choice of language, and Clara thought him a good public speaker.

But that didn't stop her from looking around the room. Sylvester King sat on a row by himself. Pippa and Edward sat together but far away from Genevieve. Will Ellis stood by the door with two uniformed police officers beside him, scanning the crowd.

Father Langford finished up his speech and then gave the congregation the opportunity for silent reflection. Everyone lowered their heads, including Clara. She thought about the two men who were dead and wondered if she was soon to find out who had killed them. Judging from Vanessa's behaviour, she was.

"Thank you for coming," Father Langford signed off.

Clara lifted her head. The brief memorial was over and the sounds of shoes on flagstone echoed through the church as people made their way to leave.

Will Ellis stepped forward. "Could Genevieve Chadwick, Pippa Chadwick, Edward Milton, Sylvester King, Anton Vos, and Jemima Vos all stay behind, please?" he called. "Everyone else can leave."

Clara made a move to get up, but Vanessa placed a hand on her arm. "Not us."

Clara frowned. She looked over to Felicity who was also staying where she was. Clara presumed that if she was still under arrest, she didn't have much choice in the matter.

Everyone else filed out of the room, leaving the main suspects. When it was only them in the church, and the main door had been closed, Vanessa stood up and walked to the front of the room.

Clara glanced back to Will, who seemed to be aware of what was happening.

"I think you all know why we've asked you to stay behind," she said. "And I will admit that this case has been one of a great many twists and turns."

"It was obviously Felicity Abbot," Sylvester King called out. "Like I said from the start. She was arrested last night and arrived here in a police car. Or are we going to ignore the obvious?"

"Is it really so obvious?" Vanessa asked him. "The first thing to understand is that there were two distinct crimes: the death of Angus Chadwick and the death of Julian Bridgewater. One more complicated than the other."

Vanessa leaned against the stage. Clara could tell that she was enjoying her fifteen minutes of fame. Knowing Aunt Vee, she'd drag it well beyond fifteen minutes, too.

"Julian has been building a pyramid scheme with the residents and businesses of this village for a number of years. Borrowing from one of you to pay the other. How else could a local village accountant have accumulated the kind of wealth he did?

"The problem with pyramid schemes, other than being illegal, is that you have to continue to grow them. The more people within, the more money you need. Which is why the Core Foods contract was so very important to him."

Vanessa gestured towards Felicity.

"Unfortunately for Julian, Felicity wasn't going to pass planning permission for the new supermarket. Felicity knew that Angus and Julian both had a lot of money tied up in the deal and needed it to succeed. She'd been treated like dirt by both men for as long as she'd worked in the village.

She also knew that the supermarket would destroy many local businesses, and that she would be in the firing line when that happened. Therefore, she stuck her heels in and did everything she could to ensure the supermarket would not be built."

Clara looked over to Felicity. She was staring ahead passively, giving nothing away and certainly not denying the charge.

"But that wasn't Julian's biggest hurdle," Vanessa continued. She pushed away from the stage. "No, before he really went into battle with Felicity over planning permission, he needed something far more important to the project: the land to build it on."

Everyone turned to look at Anton and Jemima Vos.

"Why would we kill Julian?" Anton asked defensively. "We wanted to sell; we wanted the money. He was just trying to pay us less than the land was worth. We only wanted a fair cut of the profit he was making."

"Indeed," Vanessa agreed. "I think we can all agree that both Angus and Julian weren't immune to a bit of blackmail in order to get what they wanted. Which is precisely why Julian threatened to expose Anton Vos as the man who murdered Angus Chadwick. Because naturally the man he had been in a land dispute with for the last couple of years would be the number one logical choice for the person who finally snapped and murdered him."

"I didn't kill Angus; I wasn't even there!" Anton said.

"But the fact of the matter," Vanessa replied, "is that you have more motive to want Angus gone than most people. The bitter war you two were in makes you a number one suspect. Julian knew that, which is why he told Jemima that he would make the claim to the police unless the land was sold to him.

"The problem was that Jemima had been threatened before. Her ex-husband had proven to her that once blackmail starts, it is very difficult to get out from under it."

Vanessa clapped her hands together and pointed to Felicity again. "On the night of the murder, Julian Bridgewater called Felicity Abbot to demand that planning permission be cleared immediately. Why would he call her at nearly eleven o'clock in the evening? A very strange thing to do unless the land issue had already been solved and he was moving onto the next problem on his list. As if he knew the land would be sold to Core Foods."

Vanessa turned to look at Jemima.

"Because he'd just recently called you, hadn't he, Jemima? He'd called you and threatened you, telling you that he would... what? Suddenly remember seeing Anton the night of Angus' murder? He'd previously said that he would tell the police that Anton was involved. He piled the pressure on to ensure you sold the land. Not only that, you'd be working with him to secure the shop on the high street, Milton Furnishings. The perfect location for the expansion of Vos Farm. Except Julian had arranged for someone else to get that shop, hadn't he?"

Clara strained her head to try to see Jemima's expression.

Jemima looked furious and shook her head. "You're wrong, you're so very wrong," she claimed.

"You've been seen in the Milton Furnishings store, haven't you?" Vanessa persisted. "The Vos Farm shop is very profitable, is it not? It should be with the price you charge for so-called artisan bread and those cuts of meat."

Vanessa tapped her own back. "A knife. In the back. Right through the heart. And the knife in question wasn't a kitchen knife. It wasn't one sold through ordinary retailers. It was a butcher's knife, and the murder was committed by someone with an understanding of butchery. Straight in between the ribs and through the heart. A quick and easy murder."

"We're not the only butchers in the area," Anton retaliated.

"You're not. But you are the only ones who were relying on a shop in a prime location in town, which Julian had been dangling in front of you like a carrot. Right up until the day before he died, when Milton Furnishings were finally leaving the shop and you expected to be given first refusal of the new lease. But, no. It was given to an estate agent instead."

Vanessa looked at Jemima. "That must have infuriated you. Julian, blackmailing you. Again, I don't wonder, considering it was Julian's primary business method. It all stacks up, but the real evidence came from Felicity Abbot."

Everyone turned to look at Felicity, who looked as confused as they did.

"Or should I say, Julian's voicemail to Felicity. Not only did he start to apply pressure to Felicity to approve the planning permission. There was something else on that message that undeniably connects Jemima Vos to the murder of Julian Bridgewater." Vanessa paused for dramatic emphasis. "Her driving."

Clara blinked and wondered if Vanessa had cracked.

"My driving?" Jemima asked, shock evident in her voice.

"Everyone knows you drive like a lunatic," Vanessa said.

"Whenever there is the screeching of tyres or the sound of gravel being shot aside, everyone knows it's you. Which is why, when I listened to the voicemail that Julian Bridgewater left on Felicity's machine, and I heard the sound of a car skidding to a stop in the background, I knew it had to be you."

Everyone turned to look at Jemima.

"Tell her this is nonsense," Anton said.

"She can't," Vanessa explained. "Because it's true. Isn't it, Jemima? You knew the police were hunting for a murderer, and you saw an opportunity to get rid of Julian Bridgewater once and for all. You even thought you could get away with implicating who *you* thought had killed Angus Chadwick by suggesting to Pippa Chadwick that she should leave the village. You knew that Pippa would suggest to Edward that they leave. You already had suspicions that Edward killed Angus, and you hoped that the police would pin both murders on him.

"The pressure from Julian to sell the land, the threats against Anton, the shop you had pinned your hopes on being snatched out of your hands... You snapped didn't you, Jemima? You took the knife and you killed Julian Bridgewater. You drove to his house late in the evening, saw him in his office, and then you murdered him. Didn't you?"

A sob burst from Jemima. "Yes, yes! I did it! I killed that awful man. So what? Will anyone actually miss him? The loathsome, evil man!"

Will gestured to a police officer. She approached and pulled Jemima Vos from her chair and held onto her arm.

"Jemima Vos, I'm arresting you for the murder of Julian Bridgewater," Will said, and proceeded to read her rights.

Anton was on his feet, begging for Jemima to say it wasn't true. But it was futile. She'd confessed, and the tears were real.

Genevieve Chadwick jumped to her feet. "You?! You were my best friend! I trusted you!"

Pippa Chadwick stood up. "As if you're so innocent, Mother!"

A collective gasp filled the room.

"You didn't care that Father was dead, and I found the glass vial in your make-up bag. Don't deny it!"

Genevieve looked taken aback. "I didn't put it there! As soon as I found it, I threw it away. I don't know why you are accusing me, your own mother, when *she* was arrested just yesterday." Genevieve pointed to Felicity.

Vanessa held her hands up to calm everyone down. "Yes, it is true that Felicity was arrested yesterday. You see, a broken cocktail glass was found—rather brilliantly, I might add—in the fireplace in Angus Chadwick's office. It contained traces of cyanide and had two sets of fingerprints on it. Angus' and Felicity's.

"Those of us who knew Angus are well aware of his... shall we say passionate language. He threatened people on a regular basis, so much so that some might say it became a little meaningless. But I digress. You see, the evidence of the fingerprints does not mean that Miss Abbot added the cyanide to the glass. It's my understanding that the cocktail of choice that evening was amaretto sours. Amaretto famously sports a bitter almond taste, which is perfect for masking the similar taste of cyanide."

"Genevieve chose to make amaretto sours," Jemima

announced, quickly turning on her friend. "She bought the amaretto from Vos Farm's shop!"

"Yes, but *you* made the cocktails," Genevieve retaliated. "And you've already confessed to one murder!"

"I didn't kill Angus!" Jemima said. "Why would I?"

"How does a glass vial suddenly appear in someone's make-up bag?" Vanessa asked. "Placed in a location where it was sure to be found, found by someone who has a phobia of death and dying, a phobia so strong that she could easily be frightened into worrying that her own mother was a murderer."

Vanessa turned to Genevieve. "What made you decide to make amaretto sours that night?"

Genevieve opened and closed her mouth. "I... I don't know. I don't remember."

"Could you have seen an article, maybe one in a magazine?" Vanessa asked.

Genevieve nodded. "Yes, yes, I did see something. It looked appealing to me."

"Would it surprise you to know that the article was from a magazine two years old? And that magazine had been placed in your home for you to see, the page deliberately folded over so you would notice the article and photograph?"

Genevieve looked at a loss.

"You see," Vanessa said, "it's very easy to place an idea in someone's mind. I found the magazine hidden in a stack in your living room. It stood out as the only one that had been folded open for a prolonged length of time. Folded to one page, suggesting amaretto sours as an elegant choice for a dinner party.

"Another thing that had me confused for the longest time was this announcement that Angus was due to make. Everyone assumed that he died before he had a chance to make it," she said. "But I ask you, who leaves an announcement until so late in the meal? Announcements are made before dinner or during the meal. Not when the dessert has been served. Which led me to one logical conclusion: there was no announcement. It was a ruse to gather you all together."

Vanessa looked towards Felicity. "You see, Felicity Abbot couldn't have committed the murder because she was the original target of the whole plot."

Another series of gasps filled the room. Felicity looked utterly shocked. Not caring what anyone thought, Clara got up and walked across the aisle to sit by her. She gripped Felicity's hand, noting how it was lightly shaking.

"The murderer poisoned Angus Chadwick, quite mistakenly. You see, when the cocktails were handed out, one of the glasses had a slight chip on the rim. Didn't it, Felicity?" Vanessa asked.

Felicity nodded. "Y-yes."

"And you have a problem with chipped glasses, don't you?" Vanessa pressed. "Can't even stand to see it. Maybe from an accident when you were young?"

"I had a favourite glass as a child, and it had a small hairline crack. I drank from it one day, and it broke, cutting my mouth. Since then I can't stand chipped glasses," Felicity explained.

Clara held tightly onto her hand.

"So, when you were handed a cocktail glass by Angus and you noticed a small chip on it, what did you do?"

"I… switched it," Felicity confessed.

"You switched it with Angus Chadwick, thereby giving him the cocktail glass with the cyanide in it," Vanessa said.

"Oh my god! Then… then I did kill him," Felicity breathed.

Clara wrapped an arm around her. "You weren't to know," she whispered.

"Wait a minute," Edward Milton spoke up. "If someone tried to poison Felicity and Jemima is saying it wasn't her, then there's still a murderer on the loose? Right?"

Vanessa smiled at him. "Sort of."

"What do you mean, sort of? Stop playing games and tell us who it is," Genevieve demanded.

"*You* actually led me to the killer," Vanessa told her. She addressed the room. "I heard a rumour that Genevieve Chadwick was spotted near Sylvester King's house, possibly even looking for something *inside* the house. This was presumably because she didn't think that Jemima had killed Angus, was sure that it couldn't have been her daughter, doubted it was Felicity, and with Julian dead, that left two suspects: Genevieve and Sylvester. Which means that Genevieve couldn't have killed Angus. She thought Sylvester had done it."

"How dare you accuse me!" Sylvester shouted. "You have no evidence!"

"I haven't accused you, Sylvester," Vanessa said. "In fact, if you think about it, it's really very obvious. A two-year-old magazine in your house, laid open to a spread on amaretto sours. You were all gathered to a dinner for a speech that was never given. And what an odd bunch of people to assemble. And who put the vial of cyanide into Genevieve's make-up bag? Why would they want to frame her like that? And who threatens people so often that its meaning has faded into obscurity?"

"Angus," Clara breathed.

Vanessa snapped her fingers. "Precisely. Angus Chadwick intended to murder Felicity, presumably to get her out of the way so he could proceed with the planning permission for Core Foods, or any one of the other schemes that Felicity was preventing him from following through on.

"He left the magazine laying around the house to encourage his wife to think about amaretto sours, set up a dinner party where he could add the cyanide to her glass, and then pop upstairs and put the remaining poison in his wife's make-up bag. He knew it would be found later, which meant he would be rid of his colleague who was a thorn in his side, and his wife who had been humiliating him by having a very public affair. He presumably intended to leave further clues pointing to his wife, using the variety of people at the dinner party to independently point the finger so he wouldn't have to. With such a good cross-section of people all saying the same thing, the police would have no option but to search Genevieve Chadwick's room and find the poison. And arrest her for the murder of Felicity Abbot."

Vanessa leaned back against the stage and let out a sigh.

"However, he gave Felicity the chipped glass. Which meant she switched the glass with him, and he ended up drinking the poison himself. Angus Chadwick was the original murderer."

"But how did the glass end up in the fireplace?" Will asked.

Vanessa looked to Sylvester. "Mr King, would you like to take that one?"

Sylvester stood up and looked nervously around the room. "I… I don't know what you mean."

"You might as well admit to it now," she said.

He remained silent.

Vanessa rolled her eyes. "You were blackmailing Angus, and he was blackmailing you. You were in a perfect tug of war. You had dirt on Angus' family, obtained by speaking with Edward Milton, and he threatened to install a sewage tank on his land but near your precious garden."

"I knew it!" Genevieve glared at Sylvester. "I knew something was going on with you. It made no sense that Angus invited you to dinner that night."

"It was to issue yet another threat, in the hope that you'd agree to not publish the story about Angus's father. Right, Sylvester?" Vanessa questioned. "You argued, and in a fit of rage, Angus threw his empty cocktail glass into the fireplace. Then, when he died, you realised you had to get rid of the manuscript in case it implicated you in his murder. But you held onto it because you couldn't stand to destroy your work. As a fellow author, I understand that, but once Julian Bridgewater was murdered, you knew the police would redouble their efforts to find someone with a motive. That was the incentive for you to burn the manuscript and your notes."

Sylvester grimly nodded.

"And there you have it," Vanessa said. "Angus attempted to kill Felicity but ended up killing himself. Very easy, really."

Clara rolled her eyes at Vanessa's claim that it had all been so simple.

The crowd started to disperse, and Will escorted Jemima out of the building, Anton right behind them, tears in his eyes. Sylvester slunk away, glancing at Clara and Felicity as he left.

"Thank goodness that's over," Felicity said.

"Yes," Clara agreed. She placed a light kiss on Felicity's cheek, hoping it wouldn't be rebuffed. Felicity offered her a smile in return, seemingly happy for the attention.

"I'm sorry Angus tried to kill you," Clara added.

Felicity laughed lightly. "I'm sorry I switched glasses with him."

"I'm not," Clara said. "Then we would have never met."

"How about we have that drink sometime soon?" Felicity suggested with a lopsided grin.

Clara was about to reply when she felt a presence behind her. She turned to see Aunt Vee stood next to her.

"Well, that was quite marvellous, wasn't it?" Vanessa preened.

"I can't thank you enough for figuring it out," Felicity said. "If there's ever anything I can do, let me know."

"Actually, there is something," Vanessa said. "I'd like to set up a business, with Clara."

"Me?" Clara blinked.

"Yes, with you. A private investigation agency. We've cracked the case, worked with the police, and it will help me with plots for future books." Vanessa sat down. "What do you think? We can work together, and you don't have to go back to London. You can look for work playing the violin in between cases. I think it would be marvellous."

"You want to actively seek out this kind of thing? Like, find murders on purpose?" Clara clarified.

"Yes. The odds of there being another murder in Pickle-marsh are woefully slim. We'll have to look at the local area, maybe even be national."

Clara rolled her eyes.

Felicity chuckled. "I can absolutely help you to set up a business. It sounds like a great idea. Especially if it keeps Clara around for a while?"

Clara could feel her cheeks heating up in a blush.

"What do you think, Clara?" Vanessa asked. "Would you like to stick around?"

She looked from one woman to the other. "Yes, I definitely would."

"Then Harrington Investigations is born," Vanessa said.

"That definitely calls for a drink," Felicity added.

"It does," Clara said. "Just, no amaretto sours!"

THE END

REVIEWS

I sincerely hope you enjoyed reading Death Before Dessert.

If you did, I would greatly appreciate a short review on your favourite book website.

Reviews are crucial for any author, and even just a line or two can make a huge difference.

MAILING LIST

If you'd like to stay up to date with my other work, including more from Vanessa Harrington, please visit the link below and sign up to my mailing list.

aeradley.com/dbd

JOIN THE FUN!

I love connecting with my readers and one of the best ways
to do this is via my Facebook Page.
I post frequent content, including sneak peeks of what I am
working on, competitions for free books, and exclusive
easter eggs about my work.
I'd love to see you there, so if you have a Facebook account
please join us.

https://www.facebook.com/authoraeradley/

ABOUT THE AUTHOR

A.E. Radley had no desire to be a writer but accidentally turned into an award-winning, best-selling author.

She has recently given up her marketing career and position as Managing Director in order to make stuff up for a living instead. She claims the similarities are startling.

She describes herself as a Wife. Traveller. Tea Drinker. Biscuit Eater. Animal Lover. Master Pragmatist. Annoying Procrastinator. Theme Park Fan. Movie Buff.

Connect with A.E. Radley
www.aeradley.com

ALSO BY A.E. RADLEY

2017 LAMBDA WINNER | HUNTRESS

Barista. Huntress. Hijinx.

Running from the law is Amy's only choice.

When the scatty barista investigates the disappearance of her favourite customer, she finds herself in the middle of a conspiracy. Armed with a dummies guide to camping and accompanied by her best friend, she rushes to escape the Huntress sent to capture her.

Can Amy save the girl and clear her name, or will she be imprisoned for terrorism?

Huntress is a fun cozy mystery. Join Amy on her hilarious romp around Britain as she tries to evade the Huntress.

CPSIA information can be obtained
at www.ICGtesting.com
Printed in the USA
LVHW011819210621
690769LV00011B/1397